SWAMP THING (YOU MAKE MY HEART SING)

MONSTER MATE MAYHEM

AVA ROSS

ENCHANTED STAR PRESS

SWAMP THING (YOU MAKE MY HEART SING)

Monster Mate Mayhem

Cover Art: Covers by Combs

Editing: JA Wren and Owl Eyes Proofs & Edits

For my own special hero,
my husband, Rusty.

ALSO BY AVA ROSS

Mail-Order Brides of Crakair

Brides of Driegon

Fated Mates of the Ferlaern Warriors

Fated Mates of the Xilan Warriors

Holiday with a Cu'zod Warrior

Galaxy Games

Alien Warrior Abandoned

Beastly Alien Boss

Bride of the Fae

A Sci-Fi Holiday Tail

Monsterville, USA

Monster on Board

(co-written with Alana Khan)

Love at First Orc

Monster Mate Hunt

Sweet Monster Treats

Brides of the Zuldrux Warriors

Monsters, PI

Shared Worlds:

A Monster Worth Fighting For

Mated to the Dragon

Craving Stardust

Dad Bod Dragon

Swamp Thing (You Make My Heart Sing)

Jasmine's Enchanted Genie

You can find her books on Amazon.

SWAMP THING (YOU MAKE MY HEART SING)

A swamp monster dad makes my heart sing, but his daughter hates me. Can true love conquer all?

Amina: As part of a new monster-human integration program, I sign up for an adult version of a swamp monster pen pal. Thul lost his mate years ago, leaving him to raise his two children alone. We connect in a way I'd never envisioned I would with a monster. When things start to heat up via texts and vid-chats, we decide to take our relationship to the next level. I'll move in with him. If it works out, we'll make it permanent.

Monster Island is cute and quaint, and Thul is big, gorgeous, and eager to carry me off to the swamp moss to show me everything he has to offer. Only one thing's keeping us apart. His eight-year-old son adores me, but his twelve-year-old daughter wants to toss me into the marsh—with a weight around my ankle. Can we find a way to be together?

Thul: Amina's everything I could ever ask for in a friend, and when she ignites my mating craze, I can't wait to claim her as my precious mate. But the swamp creature council will only sanction our mating if Amina meets my children's approval. My son adores her, but my daughter still misses her mom and won't stop snarling at Amina.

I'm falling for Amina, and I want to be with her forever, but will my daughter tear us apart?

Swamp Thing (You Make My Heart Sing) is part of the Monster Mate Mayhem Series. Expect a seductive swamp hero with a creative . . . (cough), tail play, size difference, a woman determined to help him form a new family, and lots of heart and humor. HEA guaranteed.

Monster Mate Mayhem is a series of standalone monster romances, each featuring a different monster and their journey to find love amidst the chaos of their lives.

Get them all:
Hot Wolf in the City, Honey Phillips
Fretty Yeti, Ivy Tempest
Gargoyle Gripe, Sabrina Cassidy
Mounting The Minotaur, Jade Waltz
Swamp Thing, Ava Ross

Djinn And Bear It, Darci R. Acula
The Naga's Reluctant Bride, Jessica Grayson
Trolling For Love, Nessie Sreil

CHAPTER 1
AMINA

Four Weeks Ago

Hi, new monster pen pal! My name's Amina. I know this whole thing's a bit strange, but I'm looking forward to getting to know you better.

I'm twenty-eight, single, and I quit college a few years ago to care for my dying mom (which is super-tough). So having someone to talk to when I'm feeling down will be wonderful.

Amina

Hi, Amina. I'm thirty-three, a swamp monster, and I understand what you're going through, having lost my mate, Sharah, two years ago.

I hope having a friend you can reach out to at anytime will help—that's me.

Thul

Ages ago, monsters melted out of the forest, the ground, and from enormous cave structures no one realized were out there. To feel safer, humans corralled the monsters together and placed them on a big island that everyone now referred to as Monster Island. Humans were allowed to visit, but monsters could only leave with permission—which sucks, in all honesty, but those were the rules. On the island, each monster controls their own society with their individual government.

As part of the swamp monster human-integration program, they set up a pen pal program where singles could correspond with a monster matched to them by a computer program. If things worked out, the humans were welcome to visit the island.

If a match was made, and the couple wanted to mate (the swamp monster term for marriage), the human needed to obtain approval from the swamp monster council to remain with their potential mate. This rule was specific to the swamp monster species, not the island in general.

I was matched with Thul, a swamp monster widower with two children. I wasn't sure how I felt about potentially being a mom to swamp thing kids, but Thul was such a sweet guy, so I decided to let fate take me where it felt I needed to go.

Three Weeks Ago

I live on an estate—it's not mine, though. It was my stepdad's, and his younger brother now owns it. Mom and I are allowed to live here. Well, until she's gone. I don't want to think about my mom dying, though she's close to the end. But I don't want her to suffer any longer.

Amina

I'm really sorry.

Thul

Talking with you helps.

Amina

We could chat by vid sometime if you'd like.

You might want to see what I look like before . . .

I'm a monster, you know.

Thul

Ha ha. I knew that already! Remember? They included our pictures in the introduction packet.

Amina

And you weren't scared away?

Thul

A person is more than their appearance. I haven't known you long, Thul, but I like you a lot.

Amina

You're not terrified about being friends with someone like me?

Thul

I'm not terrified about being more than friends with you. I hope I'm not scaring you away by telling you that.

Amina

Ha. It's hard to scare a monster.

I like you a lot too.

Can you see me smiling?

Thul

I want to see your real smile and smile right back at you.

Let's vid-chat soon.

Amina

Two Weeks Ago

I sat on my bed at the estate with my laptop open on my thighs. Thul and I were going to vid-chat for the first time, and I was a wreck. We'd texted a lot over the past two weeks, and he was so sweet and kind. He'd become the bright moment in each of my days.

What if he took one look at me and told me he could never imagine being with a woman like me?

"No, don't think that." I whispered as my laptop booted up. "He'll see the real you just as you do him. What we look like on the outside will intrigue both of us because we're different, but it's who we are on the inside that truly matters."

I was falling in love with my new swamp monster friend, and the thought of him telling me he could never see me in the same way would probably gut me. But pretty much everything gutted me lately. Mom being sick for such a long time, then being put into hospice, had worn me out.

It didn't help that I had to lock my door against my creepy step-uncle each night.

My dismal future kept me awake long into the night. I'd quit college to care for my mom years ago, and once she passed, I'd have to move out. There was no way I'd stay at the estate with my step-uncle.

Mom laid in her bed in the room adjacent to mine, and her rattling breathing crushed me. Grief kept punching a hole in my guts. I pinched my eyes shut and swallowed past the ache in my throat. She wasn't going to last long, and she was in incredible pain. The hospice nurses did all they could, but her illness was winning.

I almost welcomed the end.

My uncle knocked on my door. "Are you in there, Amina?"

He knew I was.

"She's barely breathing," he said.

I was well aware of that.

"Once she's gone, you'll need to decide on what you're going to do."

He'd already laid that out. Leave with only my personal possessions or move into his bedroom—something I'd never consider.

"Think about it." His heavy footsteps moved down the hall.

All I did lately was think. I released the air from my lungs. My laptop chimed, and the incoming vid call tugged my thoughts in a welcome direction.

I braced myself and clicked into the call.

"Hi," Thul said in a gravelly voice.

I drank in his image, though I could only see his upper torso and head. He'd already told me he was tall. Underneath the generic white t-shirt he was wearing, he had vine-like bands running beneath his mossy green skin. He'd pulled the thick strands of his darker green hair back at his nape. Unlike human hair, his almost looked like braids with soft-appearing, slightly fluffy tips. His handsome face was vaguely human-like, other than his wide, hairless brow.

"Hi," I croaked.

He studied me as eagerly as I did him, and I waited to hear his thoughts—if he'd share them.

"It's great to meet you, Amina." He flashed me a smile, revealing two-inch fangs he'd already told me were used by his ancestors to rip into prey. While his species still hunted in the swamp for food on occasion, he shopped for what he needed at the grocery store like almost every other monster on the island.

His golden eyes locked on mine, and I couldn't look away.

"Great to meet you too, Thul." Was that my voice coming out raspy? I cleared my throat. "Tell me everything about you."

His smile lifted again, and his shoulders loosened. Had he been as nervous about this as me? "I mentioned I'm a scientist."

"What do you study?"

"Insects, specifically creatures in the swamp my ancestors used to call home. I'm funded by grants, and I regularly publish what I discover."

"Do you like it?" My low laugh loosened my tension. "Of course you do. You wouldn't do it if you didn't."

"It's rewarding and interesting. I'd love to show you the beauty of my home sometime."

"I can't wait to see it." Oops. "I mean, I hope to see it someday. I'd love to have you show me around."

"Perhaps we can set up a time to do that." His words were a promise, and their warmth was echoed in his eyes.

"I'd like that, very much." If only I could reach out my hand and touch him.

I sensed he wouldn't pull away.

. . .

One Week Ago

"You'll come to the island?" Thul asked, his gaze penetrating mine. "No pressure. I want to meet you in person. See if . . ."

If we got along as well as we did when we were face to face? Which was amazing. I felt as if I'd met my soul mate, as cliched as that sounded. All we had left to do was meet to see if the chemistry was there in person.

"I want to meet you," I said. "Mom . . ."

"I wish I could hold you," he said. "I'm sorry she's dying."

If only he *could* be here with me. Somehow, I knew that being in his arms would make things better. I could grieve, and he'd understand and support me through this horrible time.

"When you're ready," he said. "Say the word, and I'll meet you at the ferry. I want . . . Is it wrong for me to say I want everything?" His low laugh rang out. "We haven't even met in person and here I am, dreaming about a future."

Did people need physical contact before they *knew*? I didn't think so. Thul was everything I'd ever dreamed of in a guy.

One day, we'd be together.

Three Days Ago

"You've packed your things?" my step-uncle asked. He stood in the doorway of the room I'd grown up in inside the big mansion his brother—my stepfather—had left him.

Only the men in my family inherit, my stepdad had said in his big, gruff voice. He'd ruffled my shoulder. *I'm sure you understand.*

Not really, but that's the way it had to be.

I'll leave you enough to get by, of course.

He had, and he was generous, but money couldn't buy everything. This place had been my home for more than ten years. It would hurt to leave it.

"I can carry your things down to your car for you," my step-uncle added.

"I don't need help." Or anything else. I laid the framed picture of Mom and me during better days inside the box. The sun shone down, and we both squinted, smiling at the camera while my stepdad took the photo. We sat on the bridge of his yacht, and if I looked hard, I could see "Uncle" Stamford scowling behind us.

He wasn't happy when his brother married my mom. At thirteen, I'd adored my new stepdad. I hadn't liked the way his brother looked at me; however, and I'd soon learned to avoid him despite him living on the estate with us.

When his brother's solicitor announced that my

mother could remain in the mansion for as long as she wished, Stamford snatched a glass paperweight off the lawyer's desk and flung it across the room, shattering it. The lawyer had been pissed off, but he calmed down once Stamford mumbled an apology—while glaring at me and Mom.

I nodded to the boxes piled near the door. "I'll carry them down to my car."

"It doesn't need to be like this," Stamford said, tapping his chin. "You can stay."

"No means no." The words ground out of me. "I'm not moving from this room into yours."

"Then leave," he snarled, storming across my room. He paused in the open doorway. "I'm wealthy. I can take care of you."

Yuck.

Thankfully, my stepdad had made provisions for me. I had my car—in my name or Stamford would claim that as well—and a solid bank balance Stamford also couldn't touch.

I was placing the last box in my trunk and shutting the hatch when my phone chimed. I swiped into Thul's message. I'd told him about my mom dying, though I hadn't said anything about having to leave the home I'd called my own for over ten years.

How are you doing?

I think about you and wish I could hug you. I'm terribly sorry about your mother.

Thul

GRIEF KEPT ROARING OVER ME, along with intense panic. What was I going to do now? I had no idea in what direction I wanted to steer my life.

It's horrifying. I'm just grateful she's no longer in pain.

Amina

This is . . .

I'm going to spit it out.

I want you to come to the island.

I want you to come to me.

Thul

THERE WAS nothing I'd rather do than leave this chapter of my life and begin a new one. I'd been a stepdaughter, then the caregiver of my dying mother. Perhaps it was time to think of what I needed for a change.

I sucked in a deep breath and shot it out.

Send me directions to the island.

Amina

This means so much to me.

I can't wait to meet you.

Let me know when you board the ferry, and I'll meet you at the pier.

Thul

Today

I GOT out of my car as it rode on the ferry taking me from the mainland to Monster Island. I was sure there must be another name for it, but I hadn't looked it up. Everyone had called it that for what seemed like forever.

I'd sent a text message to Thul telling him today was the day, and a mixture of excitement and nervousness kept shooting through me. I'd finally get to meet him after chatting with him for a month. Would the chemistry building between us through texts and vid-chats feel the same when we met in person?

This would be a trial. We'd agreed to give it a few weeks. If things didn't work out, we'd part as friends. I couldn't imagine not continuing to fall for the sweet swamp guy I'd gotten to know so well.

I made my way to the bow of the boat and clutched the rope spanning the opening between the metal plated floor and the vast sea. The salty, briny smell washed over me, and I let it sweep away the sadness lurking in my soul. My stepdad had loved the ocean, and he used to take me to the beach. We'd walk for miles and return home a bit sunburned but completely refreshed.

A gust of wind tousled my long dark hair, making it flutter behind me in a chestnut-colored flag. Pulling an elastic band from my pocket, I secured it before the wind turned it into a tangled mess.

Seagulls soared overhead, cawing, and the swoosh of waves hitting the front of the ship echoed around me.

As the ferry came close to the island, I returned to my car. The engine vibrated the hull, making my gait unsteady. I grinned, feeling happy for the first time in forever. Being able to care for Mom had been a gift, but our time had been spent in mourning due to her diagnosis. After that, we focused on doing all we could to keep her comfortable until the end.

This felt like a new, wonderful adventure, something I sorely needed.

The ferry pulled up to the dock, the sides bumping against the wooden pilings while two kraken slithered forward to secure it with thick ropes. They lowered the gate and directed cars to carefully make their way off the boat.

I followed and was soon parked in the lot to wait for Thul to arrive. Getting out, I leaned against my door, studying each vehicle that pulled in and eventually left.

A minotaur mom and her three children trotted by, heading toward the rocky beach beyond the lot. The little ones squealed and raced into the water, splashing each other while their mom stood watching them on the shore.

My phone chimed with a text.

Hey, I'm sorry, but I'm running late.

Baxi's . . . being a bit difficult.

Thul

HE HAD AN EIGHT-YEAR-OLD SON, Krill, and a daughter who he once told me acted like she was twelve going on thirty.

Would you like me to come to you?

That might be easier.

Amina

Could you? I'm sorry. I wanted our first meeting to be just us, but Baxi's putting up a fuss.

Sorry.

Thul

His frustration came through loud and clear.

No problem at all.

I'm on my way.

Amina

Back in my vehicle, I cruised along the road winding around the island with my windows down and a smile on my face, following his directions. A yeti waved as I passed him, and not long after that, a pair of gargoyles swooped over the forest on my left. They landed on a branch high in a maple tree and watched me stoically as I drove by.

At the end of the narrow road, I took a wide dirt path on the left leading away from the sea and into a swampy area with vines draping from the trees and more cat-o'-nine-tails than I'd ever seen in one place. The marshy area gave way to big open ponds on either side of the road, the water covered with lily pads cupping white and purple flowers.

"Gorgeous," I whispered, driving slowly so I wouldn't miss a thing. To think swamp creatures had lived here for longer than anyone knew. They were some of the original monsters living on the island.

Thul's ancestors had been among them.

I took the car up a small hill and down the other side. On the next rise, I spied a large, two-story mound covered with tall grass that swayed in the sunshine. Windows on both levels looked out at a neatly trimmed lawn and a meadow full of wildflowers of every color imaginable.

I brought the vehicle to a stop beside the structure and a pickup truck and shut off the engine, unable to hold back my grin. Soon, I'd meet the swamp monster I'd spent too many nights dreaming about.

What would his kiss be like, his touch?

Would he find me pretty or would our differences be too great to bridge the gap between a woman and a swamp monster?

The front door opened, and a small, green-skinned boy raced out. Krill, I assumed. He wore shorts and a t-shirt, and the skin beneath his arms was covered with thin, vine-like appearing things that Thul told me were called lecturs. Like his dad, he had thick bands of dark green hair, though his flowed below his shoulders. His golden eyes locked on my car, and as Baxi, Thul's daughter, left their home also, Krill continued to run toward me, his grin revealing tiny fangs.

When a third person came around the side of the house mound and stopped at the corner, I stared.

Damn, Thul was hot. Super-tall, broad shouldered, and with a narrow waist. He wore a white t-shirt like he had so many times when we talked, and his jeans hugged his thick thighs. His tail swept back and forth behind him.

While Thul lifted his arm and started toward the car, Krill came to a stop beside my door. He leaned forward, poking his head through the window opening.

"Hi, Krill," I said. "I'm Amina."

He looked me over solemnly. "Are you going to be my new mom?"

CHAPTER 2
THUL

You'd think swamp monsters wouldn't have a hard time finding a mate, but we did.

I did, anyway.

Maybe it was the fact that I was reclusive. Or that I had children from a prior relationship. Or perhaps my dead mate had put out into the ether that I was a bad match.

I'd tried dating, but no one wanted to go out with me a second time. So I took a chance with the new swamp monster pen pal program, and I met Amina. She was everything I could have imagined finding in a female, and over the weeks we'd talked, I'd half fallen in love with her. Would the attraction I felt for her end up being one-sided?

I approached the vehicle at a slower pace than my exuberant son.

My breath caught when I saw her face that was so different from a swamp monster's. During our vid chats,

I'd already noticed she was pretty, but sometimes, people looked different in person.

Her amber eyes turned my way, and was I totally off to think I saw appreciation there?

"Are you going to be my new mom?" Krill asked her.

I winced. I'd told them weeks ago I was talking with a woman, that I might one day meet her. When Amina's mom died, I'd taken a chance and invited her to move into our home on a trial basis.

When I told my children me and Amina were dating, that we might end up mating like I had with her mom, Baxi snarled and stomped to her room. Krill leaped around, crowing about how he was going to have a new mother. I'd told him it might not end up that way, to give her time.

"That remains to be seen, Krill," she said. She got out of the car and stood beside it, staring at me. "Hi." The shyness in her voice made my tension ease because I felt the same.

"Hi. Welcome." My voice came out incredibly husky. She was so tiny, almost half my height. Even my eight-year-old son was taller than her.

Her rich brown hair shot through with gold and auburn hung past her shoulders, and I couldn't stop staring at it. At *her*. Everything about her was different than my species, but in a good way. Her hair lifted in the breeze rather than remaining on her shoulders like a swamp creature's did.

Krill kept hopping around her like a demented rabbit.

He was going to scare her away. Or not. She glanced toward him with happy indulgence.

"Krill." Taking his arm, I gently tugged him over to my side. "Give her a second." I sent her another smile and nudged up my glasses. "He's excited."

"So am I," she said.

"How was the ferry ride?"

"Beautiful." Her smile flashed, and I noted again that she had no fangs. That was okay. She didn't need to bite me to solidify our mating. I could do the biting for us both if we progressed that far. "I love the ocean, so the trip across it was great." Her gaze darted to the back of her car. "Shall I get my things? I, um, left some in storage but brought most of my stuff. We only need to bring in a few bags for now."

"We'll help with that." I unleashed Krill—so to speak. "Let's help her, okay, buddy?"

Baxi had backed away from us, and I could feel her resentful glare stabbing my back like a blade. There would be no help or welcome from her.

"We'll get you settled and then we can talk," I said.

"Perfect."

"As I said, I'm Krill, my fair lady," my son said, dipping forward in a bow. He took her hand and kissed the back of it.

"My son thinks he's a prince," I said with a grin.

"I *am* a prince, King Hawkland," Krill said.

"Well, I'm not a princess, so don't even think about calling me that," Baxi spat out, coming a few steps closer. Her arms snaked around her waist, and she added her tail, a sure sign she was nervous. Or upset. I hadn't wanted to shock her with the idea of a new mom, but I didn't want to be alone forever. Me and my first mate . . . If she hadn't died, we were heading toward separating anyway, though our children hadn't known that.

"This is my daughter, Baxi." I walked over and put my arm around her shoulders, but she shrugged me away. She'd blamed me for her mother's death, though I'd had nothing to do with the disease that took her. "I'm Thul, but you already knew that."

"That's Doctor Hawkland to you, *wannabe* mother," Baxi snarled.

"I've got a PhD," I told Amina. "I'm not a medical doctor. Nor a king, despite Prince Krill here," I put my arm around my son's back, "thinking he's true royalty."

"We used to be." Baxi huffed. "You're the one who threw that away."

My face heated, though I had no reason to be embarrassed. "I abdicated any royal role when I joined the larger monster society on the island."

"Now that the introductions are over, I'm going inside." Baxi pivoted and strode back to the house, calling out over her shoulder. "I don't want or need a mother. I already had one!"

Krill leaned close to Amina and whispered. "Mom died two years ago. I miss her sometimes, but other times, I'm not sure I can remember what she looked like."

And that was sad, though we had pictures.

"Sharah looked a lot like Baxi," I said softly,

stroking my son's arm. There wasn't anything I wouldn't do for my children. I hoped Amina could see that.

When Baxi came outside with her brother, I'd hoped she'd be excited to meet Amina, but I'd give her time. She missed her mother a lot.

Baxi paused partway toward the house, though she didn't turn. "I assume she'll be preparing our dinner? Something that's not burned would be a nice change from the nannies you've hired, Father."

"I can cook," Amina told her. "I studied culinary arts in school." Her gaze met mine. "I didn't finish college. As you know, I was busy caring for my mom." The starkness in her voice made my heart twinge.

"I'm sorry," I said. Would she think I was weird if I hugged her? We were friends, but in so many ways, we were still strangers.

Strangers pulled toward each other by fate? That remained to be seen.

Baxi stomped into the house, banging the front door closed behind her.

"She's a pisser," Krill said with a grin. "We just ignore her except when she's nice, which . . . isn't very often, I'm afraid."

"I see." Amina sent me a quick smile that told me she thought he was as cute as I did.

"But you've got me," Krill added.

"I appreciate it, Krill. It's nice to meet you both." She lifted her voice. "You too, Baxi!" After glancing my way, she started toward the trunk of her car.

I followed and gathered up the things she wanted to bring inside.

As we walked toward the house, my heart thrummed faster than it should have been. The feelings that had grown inside me during our conversations hadn't waned now that I'd met her in person.

Did she feel the same?

CHAPTER 3
AMINA

Thul carried my bags up to the front door with Krill trotting beside us, holding my purse.

"I was in the lab all morning, but I got your room ready before I left," Thul said. "Baxi was watching Krill while I worked."

"I didn't do it," Krill said. "Really."

Thul's head tilted, and he studied his son. "Didn't do what?"

Krill's face darkened. *"Anything."*

"Hmm." Thul's dark green lips twisted. "What am I about to discover inside?"

"Maybe it's better to see it rather than hear about it," Krill said.

"Baxi!" Thul called out, but his daughter had disappeared. He thrust open the door and stepped inside. With a grunt of dismay, he placed my bags beside the door and rushed around the open living room area, scooping up the clothing draped on every surface and tossing it into the hallway exiting on the left. "It wasn't like this when I left this morning. I promise."

"Hey, no problem," I said. "I've been known to put my clothing on the floor and furniture on occasion."

While he collected what must've been Baxi's dirty clothing, I looked around at my new home. They lived inside a small hill, but the house appeared much like a human's on the inside, with furniture in the living area and basic appliances in the kitchen.

With a snarl of disgust, he tossed everything into the hall before rushing into the attached kitchen, where he swept open the dishwasher and tossed a bunch of pans inside. He added a cube to the tray, closed it, and pressed some buttons. "I, um . . . We . . ."

"Need someone to help," I finished for him brightly, following him around the island and into the kitchen. "Hey, we talked about this before I agreed to come. You're super busy in your lab and can't always be here for your children. Your nannies keep quitting. So while I came here to get to know you better and maybe . . ." Since Krill was listening intently, I coughed and shot Thul a smile. "I'm sure while you're in your lab, I get to hang out with the kids. I'll get to know them better and—"

"Yay!" Krill said, climbing up into the recliner and opening a book on his lap.

"Not me!" Baxi shouted from somewhere down the hall. "No way am I hanging out with you. And just to make it perfectly clear, I *do not* need a new mother!"

It felt presumptuous to tell her this could be permanent, though that was the goal if things worked out.

"Look at me as someone to help out and . . . we'll see where it goes from there," I said.

Thul stepped forward and traced his fingertips down my cheek, smoothing my hair over my shoulder to my back.

I lost all train of thought. Those gorgeous eyes . . . And he smelled amazing, like sunshine and everything right.

"Thank you," he said softly.

"For what?"

"For not being angry. For giving this—giving *us*—a chance."

"From almost the moment I met you," I said equally low, "we've been heading toward this. I'm not letting anything stand in our way."

"Amina," he breathed, his head lowering toward mine.

"None of that." Baxi stomped around the island and into the kitchen, joining us. "Don't think I'm not watching you two."

"You, my daughter," Thul said, his brow narrowed, "have no say in this."

Tears sprung up in her eyes, something I hadn't expected, and she whirled around and raced to her room, slamming the door behind her.

"I'm sorry." I cringed at the awkwardness hanging in the air. "I don't want to come between you and your kids."

"Give her time?"

"I've got plenty of that." If nothing else, I was stubborn. It was hard for someone to keep being nasty to you if you were continually nice in return. In addition to being stubborn, I was also patient. "I know what it's like to lose a mom. I won't antagonize her."

He nodded. "We'll find time to chat without the kids around."

"I'd love that."

His eyes smoldered. Was he thinking about what we might do if we were alone? I didn't expect to sleep with him right away, but I liked him a lot. I was half in love with him already. Naturally, I wanted to know what it felt like to kiss him, touch him, and have him touch me in return.

I'd known for weeks that he had kids. They were a package deal. If I fell all the way in love with him, I'd want to love them too. The first step toward that goal was to get to know them. If they were anything like him, I wouldn't be able to resist loving them just as much.

"Perhaps you should've considered a program like this earlier, Dad," Krill said thoughtfully. He left the chair and came over to stop beside us, looking up at me. "We've had seventeen nannies, but none have lasted more than three days. Maybe a mom is a more permanent position. Harder to quit." He leaned against my side. "I think I like you, Mom, who I won't call Mom for a few weeks at least."

He was truly a sweet boy. Putting my arm around him, I gave him a squeeze. "I think I like you too, Krill."

He grinned, and my heart turned to mush. He was like a little Thul, solemn and with a touch of geekiness that made him incredibly endearing.

He returned to hop onto the chair again. He wore no shoes, and I didn't miss the webbing between his very long toes that vaguely made his feet look like he wore flippers.

"Just so you know, Baxi's the one who spread clothing all around," Krill said. "She messed up the kitchen, too, Dad, while you were in the lab."

"Why?" Thul asked, sweeping his arm across the overloaded counter, knocking everything into the trash bucket at the end.

"Because she's a pisser."

"That's not a nice thing to call your sister," Thul said.

"Why not? It's true." Krill lifted his book and started reading.

"Um, okay, yes," Thul said, looking my way. "As you know, there's a big city on the island. Monsteropolis, which is both a cute and funny name for a city. Anyway. There's a nice, small grocery store nearby we prefer. We can go shopping tomorrow. I'll be happy to pick up whatever you might need."

"I only eat meat," Baxi called out through her now open doorway. "No vegetables. No fruit. Nothing else, so don't try to make me, not-Mom!"

"Duly noted," I called back, struggling not to smile. Baxi might be eager to drive the new *maybe*-mom away, but she'd soon realize I wasn't giving up on Thul and me that easily. If things worked out between us, I wasn't going to let a . . . okay, *a little pisser*, ruin the core of our new family.

She was going to present a challenge, but it was just what I needed to keep me distracted. If I wasn't busy, I'd sit around and cry about my mom. Since I wanted time to get to know Thul better, I could play the role of nanny while he was in the lab.

"Let me put my things in my room, and I'll get started on dinner," I said.

"I'm terribly sorry. I planned to take you out tonight. There's a restaurant on the island run by a family of gargoyles. I thought we could have a nice meal together, that Baxi would stay here with Krill, but at this point, I'm not sure we should leave them alone."

"It's okay," I said, and really, it was. "We can eat here and after the kids go to bed . . ."

He flashed me a smile, and truly, his fangs were incredibly sexy. They gave him a vampire feel that sunk through me like melted butter.

"I wanted you to feel welcome." He shoved up his glasses again.

"I appreciate it."

"I've been busy with a project, and I haven't been able to do as much as I'd like with the kids, let alone keep up with everything in the house. Once my results are concluded in a few days, I'll have more time, but until then, I'm busier than I want to be."

This would actually work out well. It would give me time to get used to him, the kids, and the household without being on the spot all the time.

"Can you tell me more about your research project?" I asked, leaning against the counter while he finished tidying.

"I'm cataloging all the species in the swamp surrounding our home."

"Have you discovered anything new?"

"You'd be amazed." He grinned again, and I had to resist the urge to climb all over him. However, a child was present. I'd only just met Thul in person, but I liked the fluttering feelings he generated inside me. It was a good sign. "The island isn't just home to a variety of monsters, so is the swamp."

"I'll be honest here." Was it weird that he might hook up with someone who was a little—actually, a lot—terrified about creepy crawlies? "I'm not particularly fond of spiders." That was a nice, diplomatic way to put it. "Snakes. Frogs. And a few other things one might find in nature." Everything, but I'd start with naming those three.

"You'll be happy to know that creatures don't find their way inside the house very often." He came over to stand in front of me, his gaze meeting mine.

It might be a cliché to think it, but I could drown in his golden depths.

"I'd love to give you a tour of the swamp sometime," he said. "Maybe if you met a few of my friends there, you won't be worried about them any longer?"

I'd be foolish not to read the invitation in his voice. I was reminded all over again of how much I'd enjoyed sharing our thoughts, hopes, and dreams over the past few weeks. How excited I was to meet him in person.

"That sounds wonderful," I said, willing to give spiders, frogs, and snakes a chance if he was with me.

The skin around his eyes crinkled. "It will be."

He was cute, in a swamp monster kinda way. His thick strands of dark green hair hung around his broad shoulders, and I wondered how they'd look in a man —*monster*—bun. I let my gaze travel across his chest encased in a snug T-shirt to his lighter green forearms with hints of what look liked thin vines growing beneath his skin, to his long, thin tail with its thick tip swishing back and forth lazily behind him. I couldn't help but check out how his snug jeans outlined his big package.

I shouldn't be checking out his package, big or otherwise. Although, if we made this real, his package would be part of the deal.

I'd never dated a monster before, though I'd seriously considered signing up for a human-monster dating service. Why not? Monsters were hot, including this monster dad.

"I, um . . ." The room had gone silent while I checked him out. His green face had darkened as if he knew exactly where I was looking, though Krill still appeared engaged in a book. As for Baxi, she'd remained in her room, silent. For now. I had a feeling I hadn't heard the last of her snark.

"Let me show you to your room." Thul crossed the living room and lifted my bags. I grabbed my purse from the coffee table and followed him down the hall exiting the living room on the right. "Krill's and Baxi's rooms are on the left side, and you and I share this wing, though we each have our own bathrooms. I've set you up in your own room, of course."

What if I said I wanted to sleep with him? The idea made warmth spread through my body. Maybe we'd get there soon.

He kicked more of Baxi's laundry to the side to allow me to pass.

"I'll get a load going soon," I said.

"The washer and dryer are in this hall. And can I say one thing?" He stopped and lowered my bags to the wooden flooring, peering past me. A glance over my shoulder showed we were out of Krill's and Baxi's view.

"Please do," I breathed, stepping so close to him, our clothing brushed.

He urged me against the wall and loomed over me in a fantastic way.

"I'm *so* glad you're here," he growled, low and deep. "I wanted to welcome you in a different way, but the kids …"

"I get it." I also wasn't eager to provide a show.

His tail wrapped around my waist and lifted me to his level. This could be fun.

Heat filled his eyes. "Welcome to my home and my life, pretty Amina."

And with that, he claimed my mouth with his own.

His touch was like lightning, shocking through me,

yet warm and snuggly, like a favorite blanket that made everything inside me tingle.

I latched onto his shoulders, liking the play of his muscles and the way his mouth teased across mine.

His soft groan rang out, and I opened my mouth, inviting his tongue inside. It felt different from mine, scratchier, thinner, and incredibly long. He flicked it across mine, and I pretty much lost track of who I was, where I was, and what might be happening around me.

All I could do was suck in the feel of this amazing guy.

He lifted his head.

"Now *that's* a true welcome," I quipped, my voice as growly and husky as his.

He flashed his fangs. "Truly." He traced his fingertips down my face.

His tail lowered me to the floor and unwrapped from around me, though I swore the tip purposefully glided across my ass.

I looked up, and the heat in his eyes told me he'd done it on purpose.

"You," I said, stroking his chest through the thin fabric of his shirt.

"Tonight, after the kids are in bed . . ."

I nodded, eager for whatever he might have planned. "We'll—"

"I find the hallway rather boring," Krill said, standing at the entrance. "Are you showing her the wall?"

"Only briefly." Thul shot a grin my way. "I haven't

shown her enough walls yet, though I plan to make sure she sees each and every one. Feels them too."

Swoon. Would anyone notice if I melted into the floor?

"Yeah, that's weird, but whatever," Krill said, turning to return to the living area.

Thul stepped back and opened a door on my left. "You can sleep here." His voice lowered. "For now." But when he entered the room, a growl ripped through him.

I wasn't surprised to find it trashed, courtesy of one pre-teen who seemed determined to irk me.

Not happening.

"Baxi," Thul bellowed.

"What?" she yelled right back.

"Get in here. Now." If my stepdad had used that tone of voice with me, I'd be scurrying to do whatever he asked.

Baxi sauntered into the room, sending me a glare as she passed. She needed practice; this one didn't have enough kick. "Do you need something, Father?"

"Clean up your mess."

"This is her room," Baxi said. "I'd say it's *her* mess."

"She just got here. Of course it's not her mess. You made it, you clean it up."

With a huff and the thinning of her lips, Baxi tugged the bedding back up onto the mattress and haphazardly smoothed it. She took the towels scattered on the wooden floor and folded them, placing them on the chest at the foot of the bed. And she picked up the wildflowers someone must've recently picked and put them in a vase.

Thul. Awww.

He was sweet.

I had a feeling I'd soon be fully in love with my monster pen pal.

CHAPTER 4
THUL

I couldn't stop staring at Amina. She fascinated me so much that you'd think she was a new specimen I'd found in the swamp. I'd only had limited interactions with humans prior to signing up for the online introduction program, but if they were all like her, I needed to get to know more.

A human male worked at our general store, and another with the healers to learn the intricacies of monsters, though I'd only had limited interactions with them.

Amina's dark hair gleamed in the sunshine streaming through the window, the light also outlining her lush curves. She was heavier than the few human tourists who visited the island to gawk at us. I liked her shape. Craved to touch it, actually.

"Thank you," she said, walking over to stroke the flower petals.

"I wanted you to feel welcome."

Turning, she strode up to me. "I already do. I liked our kiss. I want more."

Need roared through me. "I loved our kiss." My voice came out scratchy. "I also want more."

"Then we definitely need to find some alone time."

"Without Baxi snarling at us to stay apart."

"Nope."

"And no Krill walking in and asking us why our tongues are in each other's mouths."

"Or why your tail is around my waist."

I'd coiled it around her again, the tip teasing across her belly. Would she let me stroke it everywhere?

We were two different species, though matches were only made between those who could be sexually as well as genetically compatible. If we mated fully, I could impregnate her. The thought of her holding my young made my heart melt against my rips.

Her deep blue eyes caught my gaze and held it. It was only when she slid hers down my frame again that I could breathe. That I could look away.

My damn cock enjoyed her perusal, and I wondered how long it might be before we gave into the heat we'd sparked between us. Everything seemed to be going—

Someone knocked on the front door.

"Get that, would you, Krill?" I called out.

Not long after, he came to Amina's room.

"Swamp monster alert," he said.

I snorted and Amina grinned. "*We're* swamp monsters."

"Yeah, so's the swamp lady at the front door. She

shook her finger in my face and told me to bring you to her immediately.”

“A friend?” Amina asked.

“She says she’s here from the Murk Bureau.” Krill leaned against the doorframe. “She says it’s time for her to interview Amina.”

“This is just a formality,” I said. “I think I mentioned it?”

She frowned. “I believe you did.”

“She’ll ask you a few questions to make sure we’re compatible, that you’re not here to do anything underhanded like take pictures and plaster them online.”

“It’s okay.” Amina’s smile didn’t waver. “I’d never do anything like that.”

I took her hand and squeezed it, and we walked out into the living room, finding the head of the Murk Bureau sitting primly in one of the chairs, her tail slapping against the floor beside her.

Krill sat in another chair, leaving the sofa for me and Amina.

We sank down into it.

“Tell us why you’re here,” Krill said.

I rolled my eyes at my son. “Why don’t you go to your room for a bit?”

“And miss this momentous occasion?”

Baxi alternated between twelve-years-old and thirty, but Krill had been born pure seventy.

“What can we do for you?” I asked.

The agent huffed, her gaze pinning Amina in place.

Amina's smile didn't slip, though her hand twitched in mine.

"I'm Truenda Barclest, as you very well know, Thul Hawkland. For this human's benefit, I'll introduce myself. I'm the head immigration agent for the Murk Bureau. We're adjacent to the council who makes final decisions in situations like this." Her attention on Amina never wavered. "I've come to conduct the preliminary interview. You do know, young woman, that you cannot just remain here with this family without formalities in place."

"I read the information in the pamphlet someone sent after I signed up for the program," Amina said, her smile gone for now.

I was determined to bring it back as soon as I could.

Truenda's nose twitched. "Allow me to get started with the questionnaire immediately. Then I can leave and you two can get back to . . . whatever you were doing."

"Don't do anything to drive my potential mother away." Krill slid off the chair and jumped up onto the sofa, snuggling into Amina's side. "I like her more than the seventeen nannies Dad employed, and if you do anything mean, I'm going to bite you."

"Please control your young, Thul," Agent Barclest snarled.

"Krill," I said firmly. "Go to your room. You can come back out when this is over."

Krill got up onto his knees, facing Amina. "Don't say

anything incriminating and know you can plead the fifth at any time."

Amina's low laugh rang out. "Thank you for the advice. I'll keep it in mind."

He slid off the sofa and shot Truenda a dark look before going to his room. If I knew my son, he stood just inside the doorway, listening. Probably Baxi too, though I doubted she was rooting for Amina.

"Can we get this over with?" I asked. "Amina was about to unpack."

"No unpacking until all the formalities are handled," Agent Barclest said with a sniff. She opened the bag she'd dropped beside her leg and pulled out a clipboard and pen with her tail, then poised the pen over her questionnaire.

"I'm just now realizing your tails are prehensile," Amina exclaimed, looking up at me.

I leaned close. "I'll show you just how prehensile they are if you'd like, though later."

Her cheeks pinkened, and I wanted to kiss them to discover if they'd warmed as well.

The agent cleared her throat and frowned at her paper. "Please tell me why you'd consider cohabitating with a swamp monster." Her eyes snapped up, locking on Amina again. "And please assure me you're not here for the titillating thrill of having relations with a swamp monster."

"Thrill?" Amina shot me a frown. "I'm not sure what you mean. I will state that my heart flips over when I look at Thul, and I find that thrilling."

What had I done for the fates to believe I deserved such a wonderful female? I'd thank them every day for the rest of my life.

"I, of course, meant his sexual organs," Truenda said with a scowl.

"I haven't seen them yet, let alone, well, you know."

And I'd show her when the time was right.

"I see." The agent made a note on her paper. "A swamp monster male's sexual organs are much different from a human's."

"They must have some similarities, or we wouldn't be able to have children together," Amina pointed out.

"His cock will, of course, plant seed pods in your womb. But a swamp monster male's cock is much thicker and longer than a human's. He may find it a challenge to insert it into your vagina. Assuming he's able to wedge it in, you might have difficulty accepting the lecturs that will feed from the tip at ejaculation. They will, naturally, work their way up into your womb."

"I've had PAP smears. What kind of working their way up to my womb are you talking about?" Amina asked.

I started to explain, but the agent held up her finger, asking for silence. "Allow me to speak, please."

I waved my hand her way and put my arm around Amina's shoulders, grateful when she leaned into me. I wasn't sure what a PAP was, but I'd heard the subtle shake in her voice. She might have put on a brave façade, but she was nervous. I was too.

The agent reached out to tap Amina's arm with the

pencil held by her tail. "Lecturs snake beneath our skin, as you may have noted already."

Amina reached up to my arm around her shoulders and stroked one of the lecturs on the back of my hand. "I've noticed them. They're cool."

"In many ways." Truenda allowed the hint of a smile to appear on her face before stiffening her spine. "Lecturs line the inside of a male swamp monster's penis. As he becomes aroused, they twist together. This, of course, stiffens that appendage. The lecturs erupt from the tip at ejaculation."

"Erupt," Amina echoed weakly.

"They then glide up into the female's womb, where they release seed pods."

"Glide?" Amina asked. "Remember, PAP smear. I'm trying to picture this."

"Part of a male's ejaculation includes an intense lubricant. Trust me, the lecturs don't hurt as they move into your womb."

"And the seed pods?" Amina asked, her voice stronger. She sent me a look I could only take as amusement with a hint of excitement.

The idea that she was eager to be with me in this way made my cock twitch, something it would never otherwise do in mixed company. The lecturs on the rest of my body tensed and released, though I wasn't sure what that might mean. Only the ones in my cock moved and only during arousal and ejaculation. The rest lay dormant at all times.

"The pods float to the sides of your womb and burst,

releasing the seeds that will impregnate you with multiple tads."

"Humans can carry multiple . . . young, which I assume you mean by tads," Amina said. "Though multiples are not as common as a single child." Her hand lay on my thigh, and she squeezed.

This made my leg lecturs start to tingle, another odd thing I'd never experienced before.

"Not all the seeds will take, of course," the agent stated. "And I assume since a human body isn't capable of carrying many tads— I will point out that the term comes from tadpole, though swamp monsters are a completely different species from frogs."

"Ah yes," Amina said. "You don't look anything like frogs."

Truenda's lips thinned. "Since a human's body isn't capable of carrying as many young, you'll need medical attention to make sure only viable tads remain."

Amina nodded. "You're assuming Thul and I might have sex and that I can get pregnant. I'm on the pill."

"A swamp monster's seeds are quite hearty."

"It still takes an egg on my part to produce a child —*tad*."

"The advancing lecturs will take care of that."

"I believe that's my ovaries' job."

"Your eggs will be lured to your womb," Truenda said.

"I don't think that's possible, but, well, we'll worry about that when the time comes," Amina said. "As for being able to handle his . . . penis, I'm sure we'll find a way."

"Will you be able to handle the lections along the surface?"

"What do lections do?" she asked, her hand tightening on my thigh. My cock, naturally, enjoyed her touch and kept twitching. Or maybe it was the lecturs coiling inside.

"The ridged ones enhance pleasure, of a female swamp monster, that is. We're not yet sure what they'll do for a human. Perhaps you'll take notes during the act and report this information to us."

"I assure you I'll probably be too engaged in the act to take notes," Amina said, humor bubbling in her voice. "You said only some of them enhance pleasure?"

"The others secrete lubricant, something your tiny human body will no doubt need."

"I'm always open to plenty of lube." Amina sucked in her breath and released it. "To get back to your original question about why I'd be willing to cohabitate with a swamp monster, I believe your description has given me the answer." She looked up at me, and the heat in her eyes made my heart come to a halt before surging to double time. "I like Thul a lot. We've had wonderful conversations, and I've looked forward to meeting him in person. He's amazing, and I think things are only going to get better for us. As for his . . . package, I can't wait to open it."

CHAPTER 5
AMINA

"Please note there's no titillation factor in my statement," I told Agent Barclest. As for the thrill, I had to admit I was greatly intrigued after her description of Thul's cock. I had nothing against a regular old human cock, but . . . wow.

But jeez. Talk about weird questions—and weird explanations. Although, we were talking about swamp monsters here, not humans. It did make sense for her to explain what I should expect.

Why hadn't they included the description—and, *come on*, photos—in the information they sent once it was clear Thul and I were progressing in our relationship?

As for his package, I *was* eager to unwrap it, but in due time. We should still get to know each other a bit more before we hopped into bed.

Maybe I could hold off the unwrapping until tomorrow.

Thul leaned over to kiss my temple, murmuring for my ears alone. "You're amazing."

His words made my heart surge up into my throat.

"Any more questions?" I asked, eager for her to leave and for us to be alone. I'd like another kiss. I'd like to sit and smile at him. And then, I'd like to get dinner started.

"Tell me how you will address the unique lifestyle and customs associated with living among swamp monsters." The agent watched me intently.

I snuggled closer to Thul, enjoying his warmth and the way his fingers teased across my upper arm. "I plan to prepare both human and swamp monster recipes. I trained as a chef, though I hadn't finished my schooling before I had to quit."

Her brow tightened. "This isn't one of our standard questions, and I'm deviating a bit here. But can you tell me why you quit?"

"My mother was dying. She went into hospice and there was no way I'd put her in a facility. I wanted to care for her myself." My throat closed off completely. "She was sick for a long time," I croaked. "She died only a few days ago."

The agent stared down her long nose at me, tapping the pen on the paper. "Yet you're here and not back in your old home handling things."

"She was buried and there wasn't much else to do but pack her things." I'd put them in storage and when I felt strong enough, I'd go through them. Hopefully, I could smile about our happy memories and not feel so devastated about her end. "As you know, Thul and I have been corresponding and vid-chatting for weeks. It was time we met, and my mother no longer needed me."

"Caring for a parent *is* commendable." She sniffed. "Swamp monsters do the same thing. No one is ever tossed into the marsh." The agent noted something on her clipboard.

"As for conflicts, I'll address each with an open mind as they present themselves," I said.

"That sounds reasonable," Truenda said.

Was she actually warming up to me?

"Next question. As I've noted, Thul's penile lecturs will lure out your eggs."

"I'm on the pill," I pointed out again.

"*Lure* means his lecturs will circumvent something as insignificant as a pill."

What were these things? Incubus sperm?

"How do you prevent pregnancy if you aren't ready to have children yet?" I asked.

"Abstinence."

Well, that was no fun.

I frowned. "Surely you have some sort of swamp monster birth control."

"There's an herb," Thul said.

I shot him a grateful smile. We'd be getting some of that herb as soon as possible.

"Yes, an herb." The agent's face narrowed. "Have you considered the challenges of raising children who will possess human and monstrous characteristics? How do you plan to tackle those challenges?"

"With love. Any child we produce will be a mix of us

both and greatly treasured. I hope raising such a child on an island of monsters will help. Many of our fellow island residents will deal with these challenges if they, too, choose to mate with humans. We could set up play dates, and we could consider forming a group to address the situation. If Thul and I progress to that point," which we would, "and we're blessed with children, we wouldn't want them to be bullied or made to feel as if they don't belong to the larger community."

"We'll make sure they're *not* bullied," Thul growled.

The agent noted my comment on her paper and looked up. "Final question for this part of the process. If we discover that your mating was solely for personal gain, such as attaining wealth or status, how would you prove otherwise?"

"It's true that I'm not exceedingly wealthy," I said. I assumed they checked my bank balance. I had a small inheritance from my mom, plus what my stepdad left me, but no one would ever call me rich. "But what I bring to this relationship has greater value. I speak of my heart and everything inside me. If Thul and I decide to make this permanent, though I'll point out that I just met him in person today, we'll prove this together. I wouldn't enter a relationship I didn't think could stand the test of time. Please consider my character in all this. I completed your questionnaires, and you checked references before allowing me into the program. I hope everything you gathered about me speaks of my heart, not of greed or anything related to status."

The agent made a few more notes. "That will be it for

now." She sighed, rising from the chair, and tucked the clipboard and pen inside her bag with her tail. She lifted it with her tail as well, holding it against her side. "Be aware I'll stop by another time with more questions and to assess the situation. This program is new, and the swamp monster community was hesitant to join at all. We're watching matings like yours quite carefully."

"Of course," I said breezily. So far, so good? It appeared I'd passed this part of the process. If not, she'd be pointing to my car and telling me to make my way to the ferry, pronto.

We accompanied her to the door.

She paused in the opening, turning back. "Please know that the initial sign-off for your permanent mating will only be given if you have the complete approval of the council."

"I assumed there would be something like that." If we grew closer, Thul and I could handle the upcoming process together.

She huffed. "To receive complete approval after you've answered my second questionnaire, you'll only need to complete one final test."

"What does the final test entail?"

"Thul's children must agree to your mating."

Baxi was going to be a problem.

CHAPTER 6
THUL

My first mating had been an arranged match. We got along well, and we'd adored our young. If a friend hadn't urged me to apply to this monster match program, suggesting I could find a mate who'd help me with my home and children and not flee like our seventeen nannies, I wouldn't have bothered.

I'd cared for my mate, but I wasn't sure I was ready to start over again.

Yet here I was, completely enthralled with Amina.

After Agent Barclest left and I'd shut the door, I tugged Amina into my arms and held her.

"You did well," I said, cupping her face. Wrapping my tail around her waist, I leaned forward and kissed the tip of her nose, then her forehead. I couldn't seem to stop touching her. Need was a wild thing inside me, and now that she knew what to expect and she'd told me how intrigued she was about being with me, it was all I could think of.

"Thank you. She's . . . tough, but I think I gave her the right answers."

"As for children, we'll get some of the herb, peristyle, tomorrow. I'll drink it in a tea each morning."

"*You'll* drink the tea?"

"Of course."

"In the human world, the women more often take responsibility for preventing pregnancies."

"Why? Females carry the young, give birth to them, and often take on a large share of their raising. It's only fair the male take something to prevent pregnancy until they both feel ready to have young. Peristyle's foolproof; it works all the time."

"Whoa." Amina shook her head. "I'm stunned."

I smiled. "Why stunned?"

"No reason other than I believe I'm going to enjoy living here. I like this attitude toward women."

It was as it should be. I was the one who implanted the sperm pods, the one with lecturs that would lure her body into releasing an egg. The male should take this role in the relationship. "We didn't talk about having young, but I would like one if you're in agreement."

"Your first mate had one child at a time. Surely, we'd do the same."

"There are ways to ensure only one seed takes hold. If that time comes, we'll speak to the healers."

She nodded. "Then that part's all set. One child, though not yet."

"Not yet."

The smile she gave me made my heart trip over itself. Lifting her higher with my tail, I kissed her.

She moaned and pressed herself against me.

We tumbled down onto the couch, me landing on top of her. I braced most of my weight off her and deepened our kiss, sliding my tongue into her mouth while teasing my fingers across her belly, beneath her shirt.

"Yuck. Please stop!" Baxi had entered the living room.

Lifting my head, I straightened my glasses and pinched my eyes closed. I contemplated boarding school or overnight summer camp, if such a thing existed for monsters.

Or urging my daughter to go stay with a friend for a month or so.

I levered myself up and off Amina, and we settled on the sofa as Baxi came around to stand on the other side of the coffee table, glaring down at us. "No tads, no babies, no siblings, Dad." Her eyes rolled. "Yuck. And while I'm laying down the rules, no sex."

"You don't make the rules related to me and Amina." I rose from the sofa. "You're a child. I love you. You're precious to me. But you do not get to dictate how I live my personal life."

Her eyes swam with tears, and she shot a look full of hatred Amina's way. "You're already picking her side."

"She just got here. I like her. I want to get to know her better." I tried to keep my voice soft. Kind. Because I understood my daughter well. She'd loved her mother very much, and she'd naturally see Amina as someone who might take her mother's place. "I'm lonely."

Baxi wrapped her tail around her waist and crossed her arms over her chest. "You have me and Krill."

"And I adore you two so much. But you're growing up. You won't live here forever."

"So you'll replace us with *her*."

"How could I replace you two, let alone your mom? She was special. But just like I love you and your brother, I have room in my heart to love more."

"You *love* her?" Utter betrayal came through in her voice.

Amina sent me a look full of sympathy, and I suspected she wanted to say something that might reassure Baxi, but there probably wasn't anything she could say that could help in this situation.

"I *could* love her." No, I was more than halfway there already, and the realization stunned me, though I wasn't sure why. I'd felt a connection with her from the start, and that feeling had grown each time we chatted. "Amina's special, just like your mom. Like you and Krill. Like me. Please, give her a chance."

"I don't want to. She's not Mom. She'll never be Mom!" Tears slid down my daughter's face. "I don't want to love her because . . ."

"Do you think loving Amina would mean you no longer love your mom?"

"Of course not," she snapped, wiping her tears away with the tip of her tail. "I'll always love Mom."

"This is a trial period," I said carefully. "You knew

this already, Baxi. I explained that Amina was coming to live with us, to see if . . ." I shrugged. "To see if what we felt for each other would grow stronger." My gaze caught Amina's again. She stood, her hands fidgeting by her sides. "We'll see how this goes."

Baxi snarled. "I don't want to." She stalked from the room, her long, slender tail whipping back and forth behind her.

"I'm sorry, Amina," I said once my daughter had slammed her bedroom door shut. "I'm sure this isn't anything you wanted to jump into the middle of."

"Hey, it's okay. I understand what it's like to lose a parent, to feel as if no one can ever replace them. I'll do all I can to show her I'm not trying to step into your first mate's shoes."

I wrapped my tail around her waist and drew her against my side. "Thank you."

"At twelve, she must feel grown up and independent. So I imagine this is about more than her mother. She wouldn't want a strange woman coming into her house and telling her what to do. I'll be gentle with her, and hopefully, she'll warm up to me."

I hoped so. "She's a sweet girl. Give her time."

Amina smiled up at me. "I will." Her gaze took in the room, and I sensed she was trying to lighten the mood. "Everything here looks . . ."

"Normal?"

"I'm sorry. Yes."

"Most of my people live in the world that gave us our name. The majority of us still have homes deep beneath the surface of the swamp. Over time, some migrated to the surface and a few even built homes on land, though they were simpler than I've seen on the mainland. When monsters came to this island, most of the humans fled."

"I read that. They were afraid."

"I understand why. They never expected to share their world with what they saw as creatures."

"Thankfully, that's changed."

"Somewhat. We see surprisingly little prejudice on the island, and we're grateful for that. We're also grateful we have this place where we can live together until we're comfortable with humans. Some remained here, and we're friends."

I cleared my throat. "I bought this home from a human, though it was only partly finished at the time. This is why you'll find a bathing chamber in the hall and a kitchen area with appliances much like you'd expect in a home anywhere else in the country. They left everything behind. I bought the home after my first mate died."

"I'm sorry about her death."

"She and I . . . She was difficult to please. I don't want to speak negatively about her. Our young adored her, and she felt the same about them. She was a good mother." Not a wonderful wife.

"Maybe we should back off to give Baxi time," she said. "There's no rush."

"She knew we'd been matched. I talked about you all the time." That had definitely irked her, but I thought she'd get over it, that she'd find a way to reconcile it and be happy for me. "Maybe I should've taken it slower with her. It's hard to say what might've worked better. I gushed about you a lot."

She grinned. "I kept thinking about you. I couldn't wait for our next chat."

"Baxi needs to accept you in our lives, but forcing this probably won't help."

"Let's take things slower—at least around her. Look at me as your new nanny if that helps."

"She hated all the nannies, which I'm sure is why they fled soon after arriving."

"She's going to provide a challenge."

"Hopefully not for long." I tightened my tail around her waist. "I want you here. Please understand that. What we're building is important to me, and I'm not going to let Baxi mess that up."

"We'll find a way to make this work for all of us."

I appreciated Amina's understanding so much.

"Like I said," she smiled up at me, "I'll fill in as the nanny for now. I'll keep your home—"

"Our home." I hoped she'd see it that way soon.

"Okay, *our* home. I'll keep it tidy, cook our meals, and take care of the children. As for us, we'll see how it goes."

I cocked my head, and my lips twitched. "I hope it's okay for me to kiss our nanny."

"I don't want to miss out on even one of those." Laughing low and soft, she pressed her forehead against my chest. "I already want more than kisses."

So did I.

We reluctantly pulled apart.

She gazed toward the kitchen. "I'll see what I can make for dinner."

"I should probably put in some time at my lab."

She flicked her hands my way. "Go, then. I can handle things here."

Unable to resist, I tugged her close again and kissed her quickly. We parted, me heading toward the front door, her toward the kitchen.

When my lecturs rippled beneath my skin, something that had never happened with Sharah no matter how often she rubbed herself against me, I paused in the open doorway, staring down at my arms.

Such a thing only happened when a male found his full mate, but Amina was human. She shouldn't be able to trigger my lecturs.

Yet the ones in my cock reacted to her too. The tingles I'd felt earlier when we kissed . . . I'd dismissed the feeling, believing it meant nothing.

But maybe it did.

Surely this wasn't possible, though deep in my heart, I hoped it was true.

Could Amina be the one person capable of triggering my mating heat?

If so, this was going to be a problem. If Baxi thought kissing Amina was bad, she'd be horrified at the thought that I'd want to take Amina to the swamp and claim her for hours.

Nah, it wasn't happening. If Amina and I ended up together, and I sensed we would, it would be a simple mating like I'd had with Baxi and Krill's mother. Not a full-blown swamp monster craving that would pretty much consume me for hours.

"I'll get back to work and see you for dinner, then?" I asked, frowning down at my arms. Maybe I'd been mistaken about my lecturs because they weren't doing anything now. "Unless you'd like a tour of the house and the exterior before I go."

"It's okay," she said. "I'll ask Krill to show me around." She hurried over and curled her finger my way, urging my face closer.

There was nothing I'd rather do than kiss Amina. I swept her up with my tail and pressed her against the door, my mouth meeting hers in a kiss that was much too short.

"Now that's the way to say goodbye," she said with a smile. "I'll see you later?"

I nodded.

"Will five be a good time to serve dinner?" she asked as I lowered her to the floor.

"That'll be perfect." Her kisses heated me up like no other, and I loved how kind she was with my children already.

I stroked her cheek with the tip of my tail. It was all I could do to step away from her and not carry her down the hall to my bedroom.

That would go over well with Baxi.

"Later," I whispered.

Amina rubbed my arm and turned, hurrying toward the kitchen.

CHAPTER 7
AMINA

It didn't take long to finish straightening my room and unpacking.

Then, I tackled the kitchen and the living room that were in dire need of cleaning, plus the bathrooms. The home was made up of a central area with a living room and kitchen, plus two wings, each with two bedrooms, though there were two bathrooms in the adult wing and only one for the kids.

The kids' bathroom showed Baxi's less-than-delicate touch, but it didn't take long to set it right.

Messing things up was her way of trying to drive me away; maybe intimidate me, but I wasn't anywhere near ready to leave. I liked Thul a lot, and things were only getting better.

Surely there was a way to show her I wasn't a horrible person, that I would fit into her life.

As I walked back down their hall, I paused and poked

my head into Krill's room. He sat on the floor, playing with monster figurines.

"Having fun?" I asked.

He looked up, his face thoughtful. "Do you think minotaurs would beat swamp monsters in a war?"

"I hope they never war because I'm not sure I want to find out."

"Theoretically."

"Your dad's pretty strong." His tail could lift me easily, and I was no lightweight. "I imagine all swamp monsters are like superheroes."

Krill lifted his arm and flexed it. "I'm tough."

He was cute. I tried not to laugh. "Really tough."

"I'm sure I could beat a minotaur in battle."

"If you're playing, you can make the battle come out however you please. Maybe they form a truce, and no one gets hurt."

He frowned at his figures lined up facing each other. "Maybe. I'll consider your advice."

"Let me know if you need anything, okay?" I backed from his room. "I'm going to take a little break, then start dinner."

Still focused on his minotaurs, he nodded.

When I sat on the sofa, it collapsed beneath me.

Krill came running, skidding to a stop beside the sofa. "Whoa. What happened?"

Baxi, I assumed. I bet she was hard at work behind my back while I was cleaning up her mess in the bathroom.

Krill leaned over to assess the damage. "Looks bad. We'll need to call a sofa healer."

Baxi, who conveniently stood in the kitchen, snickered. "Damn, you're heavy, aren't you? You broke the sofa."

"I'm a good cook, and I like sweets. Sue me." I tried not to smile as I got up off the sofa now sitting on the floor and pointed at Krill. "You wouldn't happen to have some blocks of wood around, would you?"

He frowned, tilting his head. "We do."

"Find four for me, would you? About the same size and shape."

He scooted off the chair and ran outside, returning with his arms loaded with chunks of 6x6s. "Dad had these left from when he built the shed. Will they do?"

I lifted one end of the sofa, noting the split legs with neat cuts showing who'd played a role in the support's demise. Had she hoped it would collapse while me and Thul were . . . well, getting heated up together on the cushions? Probably. "Place two blocks on this end, one under each corner. We can ask your dad to permanently attach them later." We did the same thing with the other end, and I carefully sat on the sofa once more. "There. Good as new."

With a huff, Baxi strode from the kitchen and down the hall. The click of her door soon followed.

It was going to take more than a collapsed sofa to drive me away.

"Do you like cookies?" I asked Krill.

He nodded. "Yum, though I've only had them a few

times. One of our nannies made some, and we ate them all. She didn't last any longer than the others, but I sure miss those cookies."

"Want to help me make some, and then get dinner started?"

"Starting dinner is not so yum, but sure." He slid off the chair and followed me into the kitchen, where I was grateful to find the necessary ingredients in the cupboard. We mixed up the batter and placed scoops on a flat sheet, sliding it into the oven.

"What do all of you like to eat for dinner?" I asked. The last thing I needed to do was make something everyone hated for our first meal.

"Swamp grass, tubers. Roots. Whatever we can catch in the swamp."

"No sweets?"

He shrugged. "They're a new thing for us, but I like them so far."

"I studied culinary arts in college, so I'm a decent cook if you're open to human food for tonight." I could tackle some swamp thing recipes tomorrow.

"Dad thought we should try human food. And when he told us you were coming, he bought whatever the man said we needed at the general store."

I loved that he'd wanted to make me feel welcome.

"Maybe over the next few days, you can show me what you normally eat, and we can plan some dishes that combine both of our worlds?"

"All right."

While the cookies baked, I got out the pork roast I

found in the fridge, placed it in a pan I located in the cupboard, seasoned it, though they didn't have many herbs, and added carrots and potatoes. Hopefully, the last two would make a decent substitution for the roots and tubers swamp monsters usually ate. Thul wouldn't buy them if he wasn't willing to eat them.

Once the cookies were done, I'd pop the pork into the oven. It should only take a few hours to cook, and it would finish about the time I wanted to serve dinner.

Soon, the decadent smell of chocolate chip cookies filled the air, and we were sliding them off the sheet and onto a rack to cool.

"Eat a cookie if you want," I told Krill, nudging the spatula toward them. "Be careful, though. They're hot."

Baxi peeked her head out of the end of the hall, maybe hoping I wouldn't see her.

"Too bad Baxi only eats meat," I said with a lifted voice. I took a cookie, placed it on a napkin, and lowered the napkin onto the end of the island. "We'll find your dad and give this to him. I imagine we'll be gone for a while."

"Very yum," Krill said, delicately chewing a bite. "Amazing, actually. You're going to make a good mom." He winked, and I realized he looked just like his dad, only smaller. Baxi had slightly different coloring, from her reddish bands of hair to her paler green skin. They made a gorgeous family.

I added another cookie to the napkin and counted those left: fifteen. We'd made a small batch to start, but if they were a hit with the rest of the family, I'd make more.

"Can you take me to your dad?" I asked, scooping up the napkin with the warm cookies.

"Yup." Krill slid off his stool and stared at the rest, his eaten already. Chocolate dotted his dark green lips, and his tongue—forked, narrow, and longer than a human's—darted out to lick his lips clean.

"Take another if you want. I doubt two cookies will spoil your dinner. That's hours away."

"Yay!" He grabbed a second and stuffed half of it into his mouth while racing toward the front door.

I sedately followed, noting Baxi still standing in the hall out of the corner of my eye.

After leaving the house, Krill guided me around to the back of the mound.

"Do you happen to have a lawnmower?" I asked.

"Maybe? Dad bought some human tools and put them in the shed."

I'd take a look. The top of the house needed a trim.

I followed Krill as he skipped ahead of me down a narrow mossy trail weaving away from the house, with swamp water burping and sloshing on either side of us. I studiously avoided looking for creepy crawlies, though I couldn't suppress my shudder. I could handle just about anything, and I had while caring for my mom.

But bugs and I didn't mix.

The trail emptied onto a circular island area with a decent-sized wooden building built in the center. Straggly trees with draping vines surrounded it, plus more overgrown grass. It appeared my cooking and lawnmowing skills were in dire need around here.

Krill opened the front door and urged me inside. "This is Dad's lab. He works here all the time."

The interior was made up of one big room full of all sorts of equipment unlike anything I'd seen before, though I was no lab tech. Some sat on the floor, while others resting on one of the many laminate counters. It was a very human-appearing lab, but swamp research scientists could've worked in labs like this all along.

Thul was bent over a microscope with his back facing us, his jeans hugging his very nice ass. He'd coiled his long, thin tail around his waist, maybe to keep it out of the way.

I decided I'd just stand here quietly for a bit and watch my gorgeous boyfriend work.

"We brought you yummies," Krill said, scooping up the napkin from me. He raced over to his father with the treat held aloft. "Cookies. They're better than Nanny Number 2's."

"Cookies, huh?" Thul turned and lazily leaned against the counter, his gaze sliding over me. "Looks like you brought me a few sweet things." His golden eyes darkened with what my suddenly floundering heart knew was appreciation.

I sauntered over to him, eager to climb all over him. If only Krill would decide to explore outside for half an hour or so. "We wanted to visit you."

"I was about to take a break," he said, flashing his fangs. There was something incredibly sexy about a guy with teeth like that. I hoped he'd be inspired to nibble. "Thanks for bringing me a treat." He took the napkin from Krill and bit into one of the cookies. "Oh, my, these *are* yum." The way his gaze traveled down my frame; I knew he was thinking about other yummy things.

When I said I was coming here to meet him in person, we vaguely mentioned something about giving ourselves plenty of time to get to know each other before considering anything more serious. Were a few days enough time for that? I thought so.

I couldn't stop grinning. "The cookies are just something Krill and I whipped up."

"Amina's a good cook. We have dinner going already," Krill said. "We won't need to eat bugs and swamp grass tonight."

"Come on, we don't eat bugs and grass—often," Thul said with a wince, his face darkening. "Truly, we eat human food most of the time. I scrounge up *something* each night for dinner."

"I don't mind bugs, but I get tired of them," Krill said.

"It's okay." Bugs might be a delicacy for swamp people, and if so, I'd figure out how to collect and cook them. There must be leather gloves I could wear so I wouldn't feel the insects squirming or very long tongs I could use to pick them up.

A hazmat suit I could wear while I did it.

If I popped them into a pan and covered it quickly, I wouldn't have to look at them again until I served them. A lot of humans ate insects, though I wasn't sure I ever could.

"It's hard to work all day and still find the creativity to prepare a meal," I said. "I'm happy to take over that task, though with my background, it's a treat for me, not a chore."

"I appreciate it." He popped the last bite of cookie into his mouth and sauntered closer to me, placing his hands on my hips in what Krill hopefully took as a plain old friend way.

My hormones zipped around inside me, telling me this was anything but plain old friends. I did nothing to hide my appreciation of his body. Damn, but he looked tasty.

He frowned and reached up to pluck something from the top of my head, holding it between us to examine it. "Genus Missulena of the family Actinopodidae." He placed the spider on his palm. "Must've known you were sweet." If his wry smile didn't make my belly quiver, I'd shriek and race around the room while smacking my head in case the spider was not alone.

Instead, I gasped and reeled away from it.

"Trapdoor spiders are pretty harmless." Thul stroked the back of the reddish-brown spider with thick legs and a body about an inch long.

I wasn't going to sleep one wink tonight.

"They do possess a mild neurotoxic venom they use to immobilize prey, though they rarely bite." Krill leaned toward it, and his voice rose like he was talking to a baby. "But you weren't going to hurt Amina, were you?"

"Neurotoxin?" I gulped.

"If it *did* bite, the reaction would be mild. You wouldn't die." Thul studied my face that had to be bright red. "Take the spider outside, will you, Krill?"

"Sure." Krill scooped it up and carefully cupped it with both hands, scooting toward the door we'd left open.

I wiggled and ran my hands all over my body—where I could reach.

"What are you doing?" Thul asked.

"Making sure there was only one spider."

"Turn around and I'll look," he said gently.

I pivoted to show him my back, and his fingertips ran along my nape, making goosebumps spring up on my skin. He stroked my head and ran his palms down my back and across my hips.

Okay, so now I could barely think about spiders.

"I don't see anything else." He turned me to face him, studying my front.

I pointed to where my button-up shirt was exposed at my throat. "Anything here? You might want to examine me thoroughly, Doctor."

With a grin, he leaned closer. "Nothing so far, but you're right. I might need to look around a bit more."

At my breathless nod, he undid the first button and parted the fabric. I'd worn a lacy bra, and his groan of appreciation told me I'd made the right choice.

He stepped in so close, his warm breath coasted across my face. "Allow me to examine this area thoroughly while I'm at it." His fingertips traced down the tops of my breasts until they met in the center.

"There could be a spider inside my bra," I whispered. "I think you should check."

With a devilish smile fluttering across his lips, he slid

his fingers inside my bra, finding the nipples quite quickly.

"I don't believe these are spiders, though they're plump enough they could be. Perhaps I should expose them and touch them some more to be sure."

"I believe you should." I undid my shirt another button and released the front clasp of my bra.

"Ah," he hissed.

"I hope that's a good ah, and not an I-see-a-spider ah."

"Very good. No spiders. But let's be sure, shall we?" His hands glided beneath my breasts before he brought them to my nipples. He rolled them. "These don't feel like anything we need to be concerned about. Some-times," he shot me a heady look, "it helps to use all your senses before coming to a definitive decision, however."

Hell, yeah. "I believe as the scientist in this room, it's your duty to discern this for us both."

He leaned forward, and his very long tongue with a forked tip slid out and flicked across my nipple.

My moan ripped up my throat.

"Not a spider," he murmured. "But I should . . ." With a groan, he sucked my nipple into his mouth. His tongue coiled around it and tugged, and I pretty much melted against the counter behind me. Something clanged to my left, and my eyes popped open. A silver device now lay on the floor, swept off the surface by Thul.

He lifted me onto the counter with his tail and spread my legs wide, stepping between them and tugging me close to the edge.

"What if there are spiders in your pants?" He growled in my ear. "Would you like me to check and make sure there's nothing there you need to be worried about?" His fingers paused on the elastic waistband of my shorts.

"I believe I'm going to shriek if you don't."

"And I believe you may shriek if I do."

"Dare you to prove it."

His low chuckle was his answer. That, and his hand dipping into my shorts. He teased across my belly and between my legs, where he quickly found my clit and stroked it.

I swooned back on the counter, grinding my hips up against his hand while he leaned over me and flicked my nipple with his tongue.

"Hey Dad," Krill called from outside.

Shit. I'd forgotten all about his son.

The wide-eyed look Thul shot me told me he'd done the same. With a groan, he pulled his hand out of my shorts. He fastened the buttons on my shirt and slid me off the counter, holding me steady when my legs nearly gave way.

"Later, little one," he growled in my ear. "I'm going to taste everything you have to offer."

If he used his tongue, I'd be flopping onto the ground in front of him whenever I saw him, spreading my legs wide.

"I just had a thought," Krill said, rushing back into the lab. "There might be littler ones we didn't notice on Amina." He came over to stand beside me. "Sometimes

Dad has me strip, and he looks me over to make sure. You could do that, Amina."

"I think that's an amazing idea," I purred.

Thul barked out a laugh.

Krill frowned, looking back and forth between us.

"I checked her over while you were outside," Thul added. "No bugs to be worried about. I discovered some other interesting details, though."

Krill tilted his head. "Like what?"

Could we make him leave for half an hour or so while Thul gave me a more thorough examination? I kept thinking about that deliciously long tongue and his comment about tasting.

"Just some specimens I plan to examine later," Thul said.

Pinching my lips together, I swallowed against the lump of desire closing off my throat. "Yes, I . . . um. Specimens. He . . . put them on slides. And inside the fridge."

"Ah, okay," Krill said.

"Are you all right?" Thul asked, his thick brow furrowing. His heated gaze gave him away, the tease. "You're awfully flushed, Amina."

"The spider didn't bite you before he plucked it off, did it?" Krill asked. "Strip. Let Dad look you over really well for marks. While their bite isn't dangerous, we'd still need to treat it."

There was no way I was stripping in front of Krill. And if Thul was going to help me strip, I was going to need more than a half an hour for him to examine me.

"I'm fine." Lifting my hands, I backed away from

them both. If I remained here much longer, I was going to send Krill back to the house and let Thul play doctor until we were both groaning. "No stripping necessary."

"Yet," I mouthed for Thul alone.

"Your cheeks are too pink," Krill said.

Because I was wildly horny for his father.

"I'm okay." I told my libido to take a hike. "I'll return to the house and sit down. The heat . . ." I fanned my face. "It's very humid today, isn't it, Thul?"

"Very," he said with a serious nod. "I'm overheated as well." The big bulge in the front of his pants told me that part of him was warmed up nicely too.

Krill looked toward his dad. "I'll make sure she doesn't overdo it. I like her. She makes good cookies. We wouldn't want her fainting or anything like that." He held out his hand. "Come along, Amina," he said like I was eighty and in need of a walker. "I'll help you back to the house and inside, where you can sit down for a spell. Do you drink Earl Gray tea?"

"Excuse me? *Earl Gray* tea?" I asked, trying not to laugh. He appeared so serious.

"I've read humans drink the best British tea during times of distress."

"It's kind of hot for tea, the British best or not."

"All right, then. We'll have water."

Thul patted his son's back. "Thanks, Krill. I appreciate your help."

"No problem, Dad. This one's a keeper, and I'll make sure she's happy enough to stay longer than three days."

"I think I'll do the same thing," Thul said in all seriousness. "I'm sure there are a few things I can do for her that'll make her eager to stay as well."

I was one hundred percent sure there were.

We left, and Krill skipped beside me on the path.

"You don't feel faint, do you?" he asked. "Lean on me if you do."

"I feel normal." I patted his shoulder. "You're a good kid. I like you lots."

"I like you lots too." He blinked up at me. "As you saw, Baxi can be a pisser."

"So you've said a few times already."

"Watch out for her, and this arrangement will work out fine."

We returned to the house, and I went to the counter to put away the rest of the cookies.

Five were missing.

It appeared Baxi *could* eat more than meat.

CHAPTER 8
THUL

That evening, I sat back at the dining room table and patted my abs. "Amazing meal, Amina."

Baxi huffed, her go-to response for everything related to my girlfriend. "I found the meat dry."

"It was yum," Krill said. He was a good kid. So was Baxi. She was just practicing for her teenage years and doing an excellent job at it already.

"Thanks." Amina smiled at all three of us. I was grateful to see her expression didn't waver when it landed on Baxi.

"I'll be in my room." Baxi stood and stomped toward the hall leading to the kid's bedrooms.

I watched her, sighing. Maybe she wouldn't warm up *soon*, but she would eventually.

"Take your plate to the counter first," I called out to her, but she ignored me and kept stomping. Her door banged shut a moment later.

"It's okay." Amina rose. "I can handle it." She stacked

the dishes and took them to the counter, Krill sliding off his chair and carrying his own plate.

"I'll help," he said, turning on the faucet, splashing his plate.

I joined them in the kitchen, helping them unload the pans from the dishwasher I'd run earlier. We made quick work of the dirty dishes, and I noted how Amina stacked them in the dishwasher.

"I haven't used the dishwasher much," I said.

"No," Amina gasped, her sparkling gaze meeting mine. "I never would've known."

"It came with the house, and it's always been easier to wash them in the sink. I guess we're not supposed to just toss them inside."

"Live and learn," Amina said.

"Yeah. Live and learn," Krill echoed.

After we'd finished, we settled in the living room. Krill read in one of the recliners while Amina and I sat on the sofa, our sides brushing together.

"What sort of things do you like to do in your free time?" I asked her. "You mentioned reading like my son, plus riding a bike and hiking."

"I also like to play board games. Do puzzles. Collect sea glass and make art from the pieces." She explained what sea glass was, something I hadn't heard of before, and how she would glue the pieces into the image of waves and even birds, depending on their shape.

"I'm surprised you enjoy hiking considering your aversion to insects," I said.

Her blush only made her prettier. "You noted that, huh?"

"I've found many humans don't like them."

"You do."

"They're fascinating, really. From the time I was little, I've been drawn to creatures of every sort. Seriously, they're a whole world of their own, and they're right in front of us. Every time I delve in to my studies, it's like stepping into an adventure movie. Discovering the intricate details of a bug's anatomy? Amazing. From their multi-faceted eyes that see things we can't even imagine to their ultra-slim legs they use for some wild acrobatics; they just stun me."

Oh, no, I was gushing. Acting like the *geek* I truly was —geek being a word I'd discovered when we emerged from the swamp, though Amina didn't seem to mind. I'd resisted going off about creatures during our chats, though, worried about driving her away from boredom.

"I'm sorry." I pinched my eyes closed as if that would shut out what had to be Amina's horrified grimace and slid my glasses higher on the bridge of my nose. "Here I go again."

"Dad loves bugs." Krill didn't look up from his book. "Don't get him started unless you want to spend the entire night talking about them."

"I don't mind," Amina said, and if she *did* mind, her voice didn't give her away. "Maybe if I understand them better, they won't scare me. Tell me more about why you enjoy them."

"No, don't," Krill barked, though he grinned. "Now you've done it."

I opened my eyes, finding her watching me with interest. Amazing. "The coolest part about them is unraveling their secrets." Under her approving gaze, I warmed to the subject again. "Some can fly at very high speeds, others can camouflage themselves so perfectly, you'd hardly notice them lurking. They're like living superheroes." At least her eyes weren't glazing over like most people's did when I talked about my passion.

For the first time in forever, a female fascinated me even more than insects. I'd never felt this way with Sharah, though she knew from the start. She and I had been acquaintances who turned into friends who then decided that since neither of us had found our full mates and we both wanted young, we might as well mate. We joined, had Baxi and Krill, and then she moved into the other bedroom.

"Tell me more," Amina said, her eyes glowing with interest.

"How could you betray me like this?" Krill whined, though his lips twitched with humor. "He's going to talk about bugs all night long and well into the morning. I won't have it, I tell you!" He slid off the recliner. "I'm going to go read in bed."

"Don't stay up too late," I called after him. "And brush your fangs, plus wash up before you get under your covers."

"Yes, Dad," Krill sighed. He entered their bathroom and the door clicked closed behind him.

"He's a sweet kid." Amina stared toward where Krill had walked down the hall. "I like him. He's smart and fun. I already enjoy hanging out with him."

"And Baxi's a pisser, to quote my son."

Amina shrugged. "After seventeen nannies, can you blame her? I imagine she's built a wall around her heart to protect herself from being hurt. But I intend to pick away at it, stealing one brick at a time when she's not looking until I can slip through to the other side."

"Thank you."

"For what?"

"For not snarling right back at her, for being patient."

"She's a kid like Krill and just as lovable. She can't hide that part of herself away."

How had I lucked into Amina?

"Why did you sign on to a monster pen pal?" I asked, truly curious. "I'm grateful you did, or I wouldn't have met you, but I don't believe I ever asked."

"Do you want the short or long story?"

"I want you to share what you're comfortable with."

"My dad died when I was young, and after a while, my mom remarried. My stepdad was amazing. His younger brother is anything but. He did all he could to make my life hell."

"I'm sorry."

"It didn't help that he also lived at the estate." She shrugged. "That chapter of my life is over. My stepdad died in an accident three years ago. He had a small plane, and . . . well, I wish he'd hired a pilot instead of flying himself."

"Amina. How horrible." I put my arm around her shoulders and stroked her arm. "I'm really sorry."

"At least it was quick. He left everything to his brother, but there were some provisions made for my mom. She could stay at the estate for as long as she wanted, and I could stay with her. When she died, I had to move out." Her lips twisted. "My step-uncle did offer me a chance to stay, but it would be in his bed."

I stormed to my feet. "I'll kill him."

She blinked up at me. "I'm not saying he doesn't deserve it, but he's no longer a part of my life. I said no and left, and that was that."

"He sounds like a guy who needs a visit from a swamp monster."

"Don't bother. He's welcome to wallow in his money. It won't make him a nicer person."

"You'd be surprised how humans behave when a monster creeps up on them from behind."

Her smile widened for real this time. "What would you do?"

"Shout boo?"

"That works well for Halloween, but I wouldn't want you to get into trouble doing anything more serious."

"I'd make sure he never comes near you again," I growled.

"Thank you." She tugged me down to sit beside her again. "I don't want you to endanger yourself."

"I'm a swamp thing. I can slip into the woods and disappear. Who'd believe him if he complained?"

"I'm almost tempted to take you up on your offer,

though I'd make sure I was nearby with a camera. Imagine the look on his face!" She leaned against me, and I realized all over again how much tinier than me she was, the top of her head only reaching partway up my arm.

"Thank you," she said. "Just talking about it, laughing about shocking Stamford to death cheers me up."

"I mean it." A compelling need to wrap my tail and fingers around *Stamford's* neck overwhelmed me.

She looked up at me. "You're a sweet guy."

"I'm a monster. Don't ever forget it."

"You're a person first, and that's all that matters. As for why I signed up to be a monster's pen pal, I was lonely. I didn't think anything would come from it, but I was willing to try."

"Caring for a dying person is tough."

"You took care of your first mate." Sorrow filled her pretty eyes. "I'm sorry she died."

"Thank you." I explained about me and Sharah's relationship because I wanted Amina to know.

"Not a love match, then."

"It's rare for a swamp monster to find his full mate." I tightened my arm around her shoulders. "I'm very glad you decided to apply for the program."

She smiled up at me. "Me too."

Leaning forward, I kissed her. I was ready to lay her back on the sofa and see if I could figure out how she'd opened the front of her bra so easily when Baxi banged open her door and started stomping this way.

I sat up quickly and tossed a book onto my lap to cover my erect cock pressing against the front of my pants.

She got a drink of water and went back to her room, shooting us a scowl as she passed.

When her door closed, Amina just grinned.

Pretty quickly, we were going to have to sneak off together to be alone.

CHAPTER 9
AMINA

I got up before everyone else the next morning and started breakfast. What could I tempt Baxi with today? She obviously liked sweets, so I whipped up some pancake batter. We'd have to go shopping soon, or we were going to run out of the supplies I recognized. I'd found packages of unknown items in the cupboard and fridge, but the last thing I wanted to do was cook them. What if I served them a meal prepared with something that wasn't even food?

Had anyone written "meals for swamp monster" cookbooks? I'd ask Krill or Thul later, because I still intended to cook food that appealed to both me and them.

Krill emerged from his room and stumbled into the kitchen wearing only boxers with his cute tail jutting out through a hole in the back.

"Take me to the yum," he said with a yawn, climbing up onto a stool at the island and peering around.

"I'm making pancakes. I couldn't find syrup."

His head cocked. "What are pancakes and what's syrup?"

"Cake yum and maple yum."

"Hmm. Cake is always welcome. As for maple yum, if you say it's good, we need to get some. You know me well, Amina. You know me well."

This little boy was a mix of sophistication and kid, and I adored him already.

"My belly is rumbling," Krill said.

"Mine too." Thul emerged from the hall with our bedrooms, and I mourned that he wasn't dressed like his son. Instead, he'd topped black jeans with a white t-shirt, and talk about yum. As he rounded the island and came toward me, the thin vines snaking beneath his green skin rippled. He paused in the middle of the kitchen, frowning down at his arms.

"What's happening with your lecturs, Dad?" Krill asked. He glanced my way. "Lecturs are the lines under our skin, Amina. All swamp monsters have them, though they're more a holdout from ancient times and don't serve much purpose today."

"Agent Barclest mentioned lecturs too." Though she'd only talked about the ones inside his cock that spurted seed pods. Something like that. I was going to find a moment one of these days to see if I could get Thul spurting—and watch. "Are the ones on your arms like veins?"

"Sort of," Krill said. "Mine never ripple. Why not, Dad?"

"They . . . There's no real reason." Thul's words came out breezy, but the intensity in his dark eyes sucked away my breath.

Krill studied his arms lying on the counter. "Mine have never done that."

"Because you're a child, not a grown-up."

He scrunched his mouth. "Such is the way of life. Eight today, twenty tomorrow, I guess. I'll get there soon enough."

"Before you know it." Okay, so I was going to have to grill Thul about this lectur change as soon as we were alone. With a sigh, I turned back to my pancakes. I slipped another cake from the pan onto the growing pile, then added butter to the pan. It sizzled and popped as I ladled more batter on top of it.

"Whatever you're making smells amazing," Thul said from close beside me. The tip of his tail teased across the back of my waist.

Agent Barclest had used her tail like a hand. Could Thul's tail do more than snake around my waist and lift me onto the counter?

If I turned, would our bodies brush together?

Damn, you'd think I was in heat or something.

This wasn't what I should be thinking about while his son sat nearby, watching us, but I couldn't seem to help it.

"Thanks," I said. "The pancakes will be ready soon."

Thul smelled like fresh air and sunshine, plus a hint of all-male. It was all I could do not to slump against the counter and slide down to the floor.

I had it bad, and I couldn't wait to get him alone so I could do something about it. I'd been super tempted to slip into his room the night before. Only my worry that Baxi would find out and snarl had kept me pinned to my own sheets.

Her opinion didn't matter, yet it did. I hadn't forgotten that I'd need her approval to remain with Thul.

"When we go to town, Dad, we need to buy maple syrup," Krill said, rocking on the stool and seemingly oblivious to the heat growing between me and his dad. "It's yum according to Amina, so I want to try it."

"If it's yum, I definitely want to try it," he said, low and husky by my ear.

Swoon.

"Krill says you haven't had pancakes before." I struggled to keep a normal tone of voice as I flipped the cake in the pan.

"I have a feeling we're going to regret that." Thul backed away, something I both regretted and was grateful for. If he'd remained close for much longer, I wasn't going to be able to hold myself back.

Damn, it would be wonderful to let loose and climb all over him.

He leaned against the counter and watched me cook, which made me feel jittery. His attention kept that high heat feeling swirling around inside me. It also made my heart flip over in my chest.

I definitely had a thing for this hot swamp monster dad.

"I didn't find a coffeemaker," I said. "I only found some cocoa in the cupboard."

"That's old. It belonged to . . ." His gaze met mine. "I meant to throw the can out."

"That's fine," I said lightly, adding the pancake to the stack and more batter to the pan.

"We could get some coffee in town. A machine too, if you want."

"I do adore coffee, but I can live without it." I studied the pancake pile. Had I made enough? Probably. After the last cake was cooked, I shut off the burner, leaving the rest of the batter in the bowl in case we chowed through what I'd already prepared.

"Why should you go without something you enjoy?" Thul asked.

Well, it looked like depriving myself of something I craved—him—was an ongoing issue. Coffee felt insignificant in comparison.

"Is coffee yum?" Krill asked. "If so, I'm in."

"It's generally an adult beverage." I grabbed the platter of pancakes plus the jar of jam I'd found in the back of the fridge. Perching the dish of butter on my arm, I took everything toward the island.

Thul scooped up the butter dish with his tail and took the platter and jam from me with his hands, placing them on the counter.

With plates and utensils, I settled with my two guys, and we dug in.

"Oh, yeah!" Krill exclaimed around his first bite. His eyes widened and there wasn't anything better than seeing someone enjoy the meal I'd prepared. "I've never tasted anything like this before."

My hand froze with my forkful halfway to my mouth. "I hope that means you like it versus hate it."

"It's wonderful." He eyed the diminished pile on the platter. "I'm going to kiss you for making so many."

"Pancakes are delicious," Krill said. "Kissing is yuck. In that, I'm in agreement with my snooty sister."

"Kissing is amazing when you're doing it with the right one." Thul winked at me. Lifting a full-sized pancake, though it was only the size of a saucer, he shoved the entire thing in his mouth, chewing while groaning. "Yup, tasty."

My brain flashed to him groaning like that while he . .
.

"Well, isn't this lovely?" Baxi sneered from the living room. "Still pretending life is normal with your new pen pal, Dad, when we all know you drove my mother to the grave?"

CHAPTER 10

THUL

My heart ached for my daughter, but her words had been sent my way in anger. Her grief, I could understand. But she was wrong to blame me. Her mother was sick. I did all I could to help her. Sometimes life just stole people away.

"Don't talk to Daddy like that." Krill's eyes swam with tears. "That's mean."

Baxi shrugged and said nothing, though her face darkened.

"Join us for breakfast," I said, my words coming out as a command. "Sit. Take some pancakes. Eat them."

"I made plenty of meat to go with it." Amina waved to the smaller platter loaded with smoked lizard meat. I hunted the swamp monster delicacy and prepared it myself. The chest freezer in the shed was half full of it.

"I don't want to eat with *her*," Baxi snarled, spinning on her heel and running back down the hall. Her door slammed behind her—again. At this rate, the door was going to fall off its hinges.

"I'm sorry." I rose. "I'll go speak with her."

Amina laid her hand on my forearm and my lecturs twitched from her touch once more. They tightened and loosened, and with each tightening, I suspected they released a hormone that shot straight to my cock. It responded like those of my ancestors, though the lecturs shouldn't, not because of a human.

I sat back down to hide the tenting of my pants.

"If it's okay, I'll go talk with her," Amina said softly, concern filling her gorgeous amber eyes. "I should've done it already, but I hoped she'd start thawing toward me by now."

"Are you sure?" I tugged my arm away from her before my lecturs released enough hormones to give me a blazing hard-on that wouldn't go down until I'd been with her.

While I'd played dumb earlier with Krill, I knew very well what this meant.

Krill sniffed and stared at his plate.

"I'm sure." Amina slid off her stool and gave Krill a hug. "When we go into town today for groceries, will you help me pick out your favorite things? I want to make special meals for you."

"Okay." He sniffed. "I also want to try more human foods like syrup and coffee."

"We'll buy all kinds of things, then, and I'll introduce the human stuff to you, and you can introduce me to swamp monster food. I'll get you some decaf coffee, however. It's really good covered with whipped cream."

He nodded.

"We can leave for town after the dishes are done," I offered.

Amina rubbed my shoulder and turned back to Krill. "What should we do later today, then? No, tell me. What's your *favorite* thing to do?"

"Swimming," Krill said, his voice hitching with sadness. "I love to swim. Mommy taught me."

"Then we're going swimming after lunch." Amina's lips twitched. "In a place where there aren't any spiders." I appreciated that she was striving for lightness. We'd wallowed in our sadness for a very long time.

"There's an amazing pool beyond the building housing my lab," I said. "I'm sure Krill can show you how to get there. I promise, there will be no spiders."

"All right." Her attention drifted toward the hall. "I'll be right back."

Amina left us, knocking on Baxi's door. Baxi snarled something I couldn't understand, and I heard the door open and Amina step inside.

"More pancakes?" I asked Krill.

"Sometimes, it's a good thing to be a pisser." With a heavy sigh, he stabbed another cake and dragged it onto his plate. He added jam and ate it in three bites. "It shows strength and determination. But other times, being a pisser is just . . . pissy. I like Amina. I know she's not Mom, but she doesn't have to be. She can be herself and that's welcome in our family too. Why does Baxi have to be so mean all the time?"

"She's having a hard time right now."

We all were, even though it had been years.

"Even I know it's wrong to take your sadness out on someone else," Krill said. "Amina just got here. She's trying to fit in, and I want her to stay. Baxi should give her a chance. I love you, Dad, but I don't want to be with just Baxi and you all the time."

"I think Baxi will soon see what we do and start being nicer to Amina." I stroked his back and then we finished our meal. After, I took our plates to the sink and washed them, hoping things were going okay with Amina and my daughter.

"I'm going to get ready to go into town," Krill said from the entrance to the hall. "Do you think they have scorpions dipped in suva dust like they did last time?"

"We can get some if they do."

With a nod, he walked down the hallway.

Amina didn't return, and since nothing was banging and Baxi wasn't shrieking, I took that as a good sign.

"I'm going to head to the lab," I said to no one in particular. "I won't be long. Just need to wrap up one thing, and we can go to town."

On my way, I'd take a look around the swimming area to make sure there weren't any spiders.

I knocked on Baxi's door. "Can I come in?"

"Go away."

"I don't want to."

"Why not?"

I took that as an invitation and opened the door, stepping inside and closing it.

Baxi lay on her belly on her bed with her face pressed into her pillow. I crossed her very tidy room—something I didn't expect for an almost-teen—and sat in the chair near her bed.

"Why won't you listen?" she asked, her voice muffled. "I told you to go away."

"And I told you I don't want to."

She huffed. "Why not?"

"For a variety of reasons."

"We're nothing to you. You just met us."

"How can you expect anything else?" I asked. "Sure, I

only got here yesterday. But you and I have barely talked."

"Why did you even want to do this? It's creepy. Who'd ever want to be a pen pal for a male she hasn't even met, let alone come live with him?"

"It started out as friendship."

She snorted but didn't look my way.

"And once we got to know each other, it was a chance for a new start for both of us. I really like your dad." I didn't want to leave, but if I couldn't find a way past Baxi's barriers, I wouldn't be given a choice. It wouldn't be fair to create ongoing conflict in this family, but it wasn't just that. The council would tell me I had to leave.

"My mom died," I said, wringing my hands on my lap.

Her breath caught, but she didn't turn my way. "How did she die?"

"She was sick for the past few years. I took care of her, and I'm so happy I had the chance. My step-uncle wanted to put her in a nursing home and me . . . well, he offered me a spot in his bed."

"Uncle?" she barked. "Yuck."

"Very yuck. I'm not against relationships with older males, but nope. He's creepy and his hands wander where they shouldn't."

She grunted. "I'm sorry."

"Thanks. At least I don't need to see him anymore. But back to my situation. Maybe if you hear more, you'll understand why someone would choose to drive all this way to be with someone she's never physically met.

Before my stepfather died, he made provisions for my mother. She could remain in their home until she chose to leave. Thankfully, she never overheard my uncle telling me to dump her somewhere fast."

"That's awful."

"That's Stamford for you."

She rolled onto her side, facing me. "Who names their child something like that?"

"It's a family name. I think his grandfather had it first."

"Prissy, isn't it?"

"That's *also* Stamford. He's twenty years older than me, and he wasn't excited to suddenly have a niece, especially one he worried might take his inheritance."

"He probably thought your mom was trying to wiggle into his brother's life and steal everything he had."

"It happens, though that was never my mom." She loved my stepdad and that was enough. "My mother was kind to my uncle. Since he lived at the estate with us, though in his own suite, she tried to be his friend." One awkward dinner was followed by another with no softening on his part no matter what my mom did or said.

"How did that work out?" Baxi swung her legs over the side of the bed, sitting. At least she was facing me now.

"About how you'd expect. He was snarly and mean."

"And your stepdad let him act like that?"

"Stamford didn't bark at her when my stepdad was around. But after he died, my uncle no longer needed to restrain himself. He was mean to her even when she was sick, which was *sick* on his part. I shielded her as much as I could. I wasn't going to let him near her unless he could be polite. Mostly, though, he just stayed away, though what she had wasn't contagious."

"I'm sorry she died."

"Thanks." I nodded slowly. "I miss her very much." I didn't mind that my voice broke, that I showed Baxi emotion. "It's still fresh. I only buried her a short time ago."

"Then why are you here and not at her graveside? I visit my mom's grave all the time."

Ah, yes, there was the bark I was coming to know, sliding back into the young swamp lady.

"Because I can't live in a graveyard."

She frowned, but then her brow smoothed. "She died, and Stamford kicked you out, didn't he?"

"Kind of, though I have money of my own. Though all the possessions I collected while living at the estate are in storage. I have enough so that I could start over, finish my culinary degree, maybe go to Europe to work with a top chef before taking a full-time job. Just want you to know I'm not destitute or without options. I didn't come here because I had no choice."

"That doesn't mean I need a mother even if you seem to think you need my dad as your mate," she snapped, though her words had lost some of their kick. "I don't want one either. I want you to go."

"I don't blame you for feeling that way. But as I said, I

came here because I like your dad a lot. I think we could have something special."

"Do not talk about sex."

I snorted. "No problem. I have no interest in discussing sex with you. Well, unless you want advice about that someday down the road."

"Don't sit around waiting for that."

"Or if you want someone to bake chocolate chip cookies and keep your home tidy."

"I didn't like those cookies one bit."

I wouldn't point out how many she'd eaten, not when we were having a fairly decent conversation.

"If you come out and try my pancakes, you might like them better." I was banking a lot on those pancakes. "In a bit, we're going into town to get supplies. I want to cook things I enjoy to share with you, your dad, and your little brother, but I also want to learn how to prepare the swamp monster dishes you like."

"Why bother? Maybe it won't work out between you and my dad."

"I think it will."

She growled. "You barely know him."

"Which is why we're talking, interacting together."

Her head tilted, and she watched my face. "Why do you like him?"

"Because he's good to you and your brother. He's smart and interesting to talk to." He was also a great kisser. A geeky, sweet guy who loved insects and made me almost want to trot over to his lab and ask him to show them all to me. For a woman who would shriek and shiver if a ladybug landed on her arm, that was a big step forward. "He's cute too." He wore t-shirts and jeans very well.

"Yuck." Her nose wrinkled. "Don't tell me that. This makes it sound like I'm going to be stuck with you forever."

"Actually, no."

She frowned. "Why not? You just said you find him cute and kind. I see the way you look at him."

"Even if I like him a lot or even fall in love with him, I'm not someone who'll step between you and your dad. If you still hate me, I'll have to leave." Maybe I was foolish to offer her this weapon, but I meant it. I wasn't going to be with Thul if I had to wage a war every day I lived in this house.

Did she know she was going to have to give the final approval? I wasn't sure if I should tell her that.

"You'd really leave?" She was clearly skeptical.

"Yup. If it helps, you could look at me as your new nanny for now. One who might or might not step into a stepmother role."

"Did you hate your stepfather at first?"

I smiled sadly at the memory. "Nope. I mean, I'm sure I was nervous about him. Lots of times, new stepparents don't want to have anything to do with kids that come with the relationship, but he saw us as a package deal. He loved my mom, so that meant he was eager to know me, to love me."

"I can't see you loving me."

"Why not? I'm sure under all those snarls, you're a lovable person."

She snorted.

"My goal while getting to know you, your dad, and your brother is to take care of your house. While you're essentially grown up, your brother's still too young to be on his own while your dad works, don't you think?"

"I can watch him."

"Do you want to do that all the time? I guess I get it. It's like me caring for my mom. I loved her so much. I wish I could've done more for her. I wish I could've helped her get better."

"Nothing made my mom better. We cooked her favorite foods, stroked her back, and Dad would sit beside her, holding her hand. But nothing made a difference." She sniffed and wiped her eyes.

"It was the same with me and my mom." The tightness in my throat just wouldn't leave no matter how hard I swallowed.

"My brother *can* be a pain in the tail," Baxi finally said.

That was a matter of perspective, and honestly, that was *her* current role, not his.

"Maybe since you don't need a mom, and it sounds like you don't think you need a nanny either, we can be friends," I said.

"Don't push yourself on me. Please." A scowl took over her sad expression.

I rose, figuring I'd planted enough seeds. Now I needed to give them a chance to grow. It was hard to hate someone you sympathized with, though I hadn't told her about my mom for that reason. The grief I carried was such a burden. It helped to share it with others even if the person pretty much hated you.

"This afternoon, your brother and I are going swimming." I paused at her door. "You're welcome to join us. Or not. Same with going into town. Maybe you've got things you'd rather do here."

I left and went out to the kitchen, finding Krill sitting on the chair in the living room, reading a book.

Thul was nowhere to be found.

"I'm ready to go into town," Krill said, looking up.

"Where's your dad?"

He shrugged. "Went to work, I guess."

"All right, then. We know where to find him. When we get back from town, we can plan dinner."

"And go swimming."

"Definitely swimming."

When I opened the front door, I found Thul coming along the path around the front of the house.

"Ready to go?" he asked, waving to the truck parked in the driveway.

"Sure."

"Baxi, you coming with us?" he called out.

"Go away!"

Worry snarled in my belly, but there wasn't anything I could do about it.

"It's okay to leave her?" I asked, staring toward her bedroom.

"We won't be gone long," Thul said. He looked Krill's way. "Ready to go?"

Krill grinned. "More than."

We climbed inside, Krill settling in the back, and we headed into town.

CHAPTER 12

THUL

"Buy whatever you want," I told Amina as we took a cart—a human thing but so easy to use—and headed into the store. "When we first emerged from the swamp, the store only carried items that would appeal to humans."

"That must've been tough."

"My ancestors ate swamp grasses, fish, and frogs, plus dug tubers along the shore. Bugs, naturally too. Lizards, and a variety of other aquatic creatures. We weren't used to bread, canned items, or the idea of buying meat in packages."

I didn't miss her wince when I mentioned insects.

"Would you like me to prepare bugs, frogs, and tubers for you?" she asked.

"Honestly, I've been enjoying what you've been making already. We've experimented with some human foods, and we enjoy them. If I get a longing for what my mom might've prepared, I'll make it myself or we can do that together."

"That would be fun."

"I'll help too," Krill said. "I can catch the frogs."

I had to hand it to Amina; her smile didn't waver a bit, though her voice came out a little shrill. "Sounds great."

While Krill pushed the cart, we went up and down the aisles, Amina adding various ingredients, some I'd seen but hadn't considered trying before. She paused in the aisle with items specific to swamp creatures in general. Yetis enjoyed what we did, as did the alligator and croc shifters.

"Let's take a look, shall we?" She started slowly down the aisle, stopping to pick up a package of dried frog's legs. "Look, Krill. No need for you to go hunting. We could use these." She placed them in the cart and continued onward.

I loved how brave and confident she was about this.

"I like catching frogs," Krill said. "They're slippery and if I squish them, they pop out of the top of my hand."

"Don't talk about frog torture, please," I hissed.

Krill rolled his eyes. "I ask them before I do it."

"You talk to frogs but still eat them?" Amina asked.

"I get hungry." Krill pointed to a container of snail slime sauce. "Can we get some of that? It would've been yum on Amina's pork roast yesterday."

"Sure." I could afford whatever he wanted. My research was so specialized, it paid well. And since I owned my home, I had few expenses.

"Tadpole soup starter." Amina stared down at the package; her face neutral.

All my life, I'd been proud of my heritage. Swamp people were respected in the monster community. It had never occurred to me to be embarrassed by how we behaved or what we ate. A twinge of something I couldn't define shot through me, and I braced myself for her reaction.

"Can we get this?" she asked happily. "The recipe on the back looks interesting. We'll need cattail stalks too."

That feeling slipped away like it had never been there. "Yes."

"I'm not usually the adventurous type." Her eyes flashed with humor. "But this sounds good. And if you guys like it, I want to make it."

"You don't have to eat anything you're not excited about," I said carefully.

"I don't like spiders. You've seen that already." She tossed the package into the cart. "But you're not asking me to eat them—yet."

"We don't eat spiders," Krill said seriously. "Who would?"

"Exactly." She shot him a grin. "Who would?"

With that, she continued down the aisle, picking out various items and, with my nod, placing them in the cart. We added things from the human aisle, but we didn't shop only there. She was intrigued by the forest mushrooms and moss commonly consumed by my minotaur friends, plus a brew made from swamp weeds that gargoyles adored.

"Salt and vinegar cattail crips." She held up two packages for Krill to choose from. "Or would you rather have the barbecue flavor?"

"Barbecue is yum." He leaned against my side, and she turned and continued studying the items on the shelves. "I like her, Dad." He made no effort to lower his voice. "Can we keep her?"

"Definitely," I growled.

My lecturs started rippling again.

Turning back, she frowned and traced her fingertip across one.

That made my cock jerk, slamming against my jeans.

Soon, I was going to have to tell Amina she was driving me into my mating heat.

CHAPTER 13
AMINA

W hen it started to rain on the way home, we opted not to go swimming.

"Tomorrow," I said. "I promise."

Krill nodded and smiled, skipping into the house with his arms loaded with grocery bags.

After we put everything away, Thul went to his lab, and me and Krill put together a puzzle on the dining room table. Baxi hovered in the living room, a book open on her lap, though she didn't turn the pages. She also didn't get up and help us put the puzzle together, but she kept looking our way. At least she wasn't hiding in her room.

I made the tadpole stew that night and while I was a bit squeamish (inside, 'cause I'd never show it) about what went into it—tadpoles? —I tried it. It tasted amazing, and I finished my bowl. We ate it with a loaf of banana bread, which was my mom's recipe. A nice combination of both our worlds.

Baxi ate without complaining, a step up for sure. She scowled but tasted the banana bread, and while she pushed her plate away with scorn after only one nibble, I noted she slipped the slice into her napkin when we were finished and suddenly *had to go to her room*, taking it with her. That little sneak.

I'd have to make more cookies and leave them on the counter. Everyone said a way to a man's heart was through his stomach, and that might apply to potential stepdaughters as well.

When I went out to the kitchen the next morning, I found Thul sitting at the counter, reading. There was something incredibly sexy about a guy with a book. It hit that same part of my heart that tingled when I saw a cute guy cooing to a baby.

"Take me to the coffee," I said in my best zombie voice. Which brought a question to mind. "Are zombies real?"

He looked up from his book. "Not as far as I know."

"Good. Good." I tugged the coffeemaker we'd bought the day before from the box, rinsed it out, and got a pot going. Soon, the yummy scent of smoked ground beans filled the air, and if I sucked the smell in hard enough, it just might transfer to my veins.

I got out a mug and the cream, and after dumping water into the top of the pot, I turned to lean against the counter, finding Thul studying me more than his book.

"Whatcha reading?" I asked.

"Morphological and Structural Analysis of Coleopteran Elytra: Unveiling the Spectral Complexity."

"And in English?"

His thick brow lined with lecturs scrunched together before it. A smile that sparked a low simmer in my belly curled up on the left corner of his mouth. "The study and analysis of beetle wings."

"An entire book all about beetle wings?"

"It's quite fascinating."

It probably was, though not a book I would check out of the library.

His gaze traveled down my frame, and that simmer he'd started turned into a rolling boil.

"You look nice today," he said, color flooding his face.

"Thanks." I glanced down at the jeans and oversized t-shirt I'd dragged on after a quick shower. At least I'd combed my hair.

"You always do." His face darkened even more.

Being with him felt refreshing. We were still sounding each other out, but there was no denying we had chemistry. Part of me was ready to drag him off to bed, but another part of me liked that we were taking this slowly. Sort of slowly.

Okay, not slowly. He'd had my nipple in his mouth and his hand down my shorts yesterday. But I hadn't orgasmed. That must count for going slow.

He was interesting to talk to and fun to hang around with.

He was someone I could love.

Actually, he was someone I was in love with already. The feeling swam into me when we'd vid-chatted, and it had settled in for the long haul over the past few days.

"Are you all right?" he asked softly, dragging his gaze away from me. I liked it there. It made my skin tingle and . . .

I frowned. "Your lecturs are dancing again."

His laugh was low. "Dancing. I like that. Yeah, they're doing it again." He lifted his arms where the vine-like things beneath his skin were swarming, rippling, and snapping.

My breath caught. "It doesn't mean you're sick or something, does it?"

"It means I'm healthy. Fertile."

Now that was a new one. "Fertile?"

He sucked in a deep breath. "When a swamp person meets their full mate, a chemical reaction occurs deep inside them, and this is the result."

"This has to do with your . . . inner lecturs, doesn't it?"

He nodded. "I hope it's okay that you've triggered them, though I'm not sure what I'll do if you say it repulses you."

"It's kind of a turn on."

His eyes smoldered.

"You said full mate?" I said. "I assume you mean me, but I'm human."

"I don't believe that matters."

"Hmm."

"As you must suspect, we're always fertile to some extent, or I wouldn't have Baxi and Krill, but now . . ."

I waited in silence, holding my breath, because I had to hear what he'd say next.

"This means I could plant my seed pods inside you at any time, Amina, and you'd soon be carrying my young. I'm entering my mating heat."

"Heat," I was repeating him, but to say I was stunned was an understatement.

"It means I want to fuck you for hours."

"Hours," I sighed, nearly sliding to the floor.

That, I could get into. "This means you want lots of sex."

"Yup."

"And we didn't stop at the healer for herbs."

"I threw out what I had left years ago." His tail whipped around my waist, and he stepped in front of me to shield my body while the tip of his tail slid down the front of my shorts and between my legs.

"No cock until there are herbs," I said. "That's my assumption, anyway."

"My poor cock." He flashed his fangs my way.

I slumped back against the counter in a swoon. "How long will it take for you to visit the healer?"

"I'll do it as soon as she returns from visiting her family."

"When's that?"

"Tomorrow or the day after that."

"Your cock will be lonely."

His smile widened. "Perhaps, but I bet my tail will enjoy getting to know you better." Leaning forward, he flicked his long tongue across the lobe of my ear while his tail did the same with my clit. It found it even through my shorts. "What do you say, full mate?"

"I say that we need to test out your theory very soon, Dr. Hawkland."

CHAPTER 14
THUL

My cock-blocking kids started snarling about who would get the bathroom first before I could give Amina more than a hint about what I was going to do with my tail.

"Use mine," I bellowed, backing away from Amina.

She sucked in a breath and stepped away to putter with something on the counter while Krill scooted down the hall and into my bathroom. The sound of the shower soon rang out.

Pain shot from my fingers, and I lifted my hands, staring in shock as lecturs erupted from my fingertips and fused together, forming thin bands resembling the swamp grass my people were named from. They coalesced into one thick strand still connected to me, streaming toward my full mate.

I'd heard of this but never believed it could be true.

"What's happening?" Amina moved toward me when almost all women would flee. "Are you okay?"

"They're . . ." Heat poured through me, centering in my cock, and it stiffened even further.

The thick bands coiled around her abdomen. Her hands lifted, and she stared wide-eyed down at my lectur limbs that were already tugging her close until she was pressed flush against me.

"Whoa!"

I lifted her onto a clear section of the countertop and stepped up to her, my lecturs retracting somewhat, though still keeping her bound to me. She gaped up at me. "I . . ."

"You smell amazing," I growled. "Do you taste as wonderful, my precious mate?"

"When did the Thul I'm coming to love turn into this unbelievably sexy swamp god?"

"You've ignited my lecturs. Me."

"You're geeky." She tapped the side of my glasses. "A scientist lost in your research."

Overcome by the hormones charging through me, I ripped off my glasses and tossed them aside. My shirt followed, and it was all I could do not to shred my pants and reveal my cock.

"I . . ." She swallowed a gulp and peered up at me through her lashes. "I like the geeky Thul, but this one's incredibly attractive too. However . . ."

Leaning close, I traced my lips up her neck and growled near her ear. "You will be mine."

"Do you think they'll notice if we sneak away right now for you to show me more of what your tail can do?" A dare came through in her voice. Her hands latched onto my shoulders and kneaded. "I know I can't have cock, but I'm more than willing to take you up on your tail offer."

We had maybe five minutes before my young were done bathing and dressed.

I stroked her face with the backs of my knuckles, and when her lips parted, I kissed her.

She moaned and tugged me close, her legs parting and hitching onto my hips.

I softened my mouth, refusing to give in to the wildness threatening to consume me. It would be easy to let go, to lay her back on the counter, shred her clothing, and plunge my cock inside her. I'd drive myself into her over and over until she shuddered beneath me. Only then would I come, releasing the lecturs packed with translucent pods that would explode in her womb and lure out her eggs. It wouldn't be long after that before her fertilized tads would implant in her womb.

The tips of my finger lecturs traced up and down her sides, slowly moving toward her breasts. The lectur tips were highly sensitive, and when I slipped them beneath her shirt and encountered her overheated skin, liquid fire shot through me.

She placed her palms on my chest. My skin flamed, and when she teased her fingertips across my nipples, it was all I could do not to come right then and there.

"I smell something burning." The voice came from the hall, penetrating my consciousness and bringing me back to the present.

I lifted my head, and Amina stared up at me with limpid eyes, her lips swollen from mine.

"Krill's coming," she whispered.

"Do you think he'd notice us kissing?"

Her smile created dimples in her cheeks. "He might. He *would* notice your lecturs on my breasts."

"What's burning, by the way?"

"Burning . . ." Her brow knit together before her face cleared. "Shit. I forgot to put the coffeepot on the burner."

Water hissed and steamed, and an odd, smoky smell filled the air.

Before Krill could round the counter, we fixed our clothing and put some distance between us. My lecturs retracted back inside my hands, thankfully. I wasn't sure how I'd explain them to my son.

I grabbed a towel, tossing it onto the pool of brown water steaming on the counter.

Amina yanked the cord from the wall, and the red light on the new device extinguished. "I'll clean this up and start over."

"I'll help."

Krill came around the island and leaned his back against it. "If this is a human dish you plan to serve for breakfast, Amina, I believe I'd prefer pancakes."

"Nope." She sent him an indulgent smile that heated when it traveled across me "I planned to make cinnamon muffins and ground gator skin sausage."

"Yum," Krill said with a grin. He climbed onto a stool

and leaned his arms on the counter. "You may serve this delightful dish at any time."

"I'm afraid the muffins might take a little time to make, though the sausage won't. How about gator egg omelets instead to go with it?"

"Double yum."

I took the sponge and mopped up the mess while she created her beverage once more, this time placing the glass container beneath the spout that had spit out the drink.

My lecturs wouldn't remain retracted for long. She'd sparked something inside me that wasn't going to stop churning until I felt her shuddering in ecstasy beneath me.

"As for you." Amina sidled up to me. She placed my glasses back on my face, making me realize I wasn't even wearing them, and tugged my shirt down, smoothing the hem. "I believe we'll need to finish our conversation later. I'd like to hear more. So much more."

CHAPTER 15
AMINA

I wasn't sure what had come over me. If Thul had shoved my shorts down and tugged me to the edge of the counter, I would've let him do whatever he pleased with my body.

There was nothing wrong with that except the kids could've walked in right in the middle.

I still wanted him to do whatever he pleased with me. But Krill was here, and he was a sweet little boy. No need to shock him with his parents' antics.

Ah . . . My grin made my cheeks ache.

Parents with an S?

I did sort of see him as a son. If we made this permanent, he'd be my stepson, but a woman didn't have to give birth to a child to love him with her whole heart, to feel like he was hers.

"I'm going to hold you to that promise," Thul said in that low growly voice that made my ovaries explode.

There was no need for him to deploy lectur-lure. They were churning out the eggs already.

We needed to have a talk not only about seed pods, but about where he saw this going between us.

After giving him a look loaded with promise, I got out the frying pan and the gator eggs, plus the sausage. In no time, a wonderful smell filled the kitchen, shoving aside the hint of smokey-scorched coffee lingering in the air.

I poured a cup, added cream, and took a sip before flipping the eggs frying in the butter. When they were done, I slid them onto a platter and cooked more. My guys had big appetites, and no one left my kitchen hungry.

"Human food?" Baxi asked from the living room.

"Gator parts and pieces for breakfast," I said cheerfully, sending her a smile she didn't return, though she didn't scowl. "Good morning."

She huffed and sank onto one of the stools at the island.

Thul closed his book and walked over to the coffeemaker. I tried to focus on my cooking and not the way his tail glided out and teased the back of my calf.

Something explosive was happening between us. Was the full mate thing related? I was human; I wasn't capable of whatever chemical reaction might happen between a full mate swamp monster couple. But it looked like me not being swampy didn't matter.

We ate—even Baxi—and took care of the dishes.

"I'm heading to my lab." Thul ran a fingertip down my arm, and I could tell he wanted to kiss me. Maybe let his lecturs loose once more. I was curious to find out what they and his tail might be capable of doing sexually. Swamp monster sex was a new, though very exciting, notion for me.

It looked like I'd have to wait to find out. It was time to be a stepmom. Later, Thul and I were going to find some time where we could explore everything he had to offer.

Well, except his cock. As horny as my ovaries felt, I wasn't sure it was time to create any new tads. Not until we'd been given final approval for our mating. Which took me back to Baxi and her ongoing snarls. Would she ever relent?

Thul left, and Krill raced to his room. "I'll be ready to go swimming soon!" In no time, he returned wearing swim shorts and his feet bare. "I'm ready."

Shaking my head, I grinned. "You're fast. Let me grab my things and put on my suit, and we'll go."

He nodded, mumbling around a bite of the cookies I'd made the night before. That kid could eat enough for a minotaur. "Be fast."

AFTER GRABBING a few towels and dressing in my swimsuit and a sundress, I packed sandwiches and a jug of water in a basket.

Then I went down the hall and knocked on Baxi's door. "Hey. Me and Krill are going swimming. Want to come with us?"

"No," she said sullenly. She was probably mad that

she'd eaten a ton of what I'd prepared for breakfast. Defection in its finest form was sinking into her pores, and she was going to avoid me to punish me for being the one to deliver her downfall.

"You're sure?"

"Go away."

"If you change your mind, you're welcome. You know where the swimming hole is, right?"

"Yes," she growled. "Leave. Please!"

"I mean it. We're going to have fun. We've got a picnic lunch and drinks, and I made enough for you. We might make up some games while we're there. Come join us if you change your mind."

Maybe I was being too sunny, but I liked her despite her snarls. I did want her to join us.

When she barked out another no, Krill and I left, me carrying towels and him our picnic lunch.

We took the same trail through the swamp and emerged on the island with Thul's lab.

I wanted to go inside. Maybe sit with him a bit and chat.

Nah, no sitting unless it was on top of him, though cock was out of the picture for now. Maybe he could put me on the counter and show me what his tongue could do between my legs.

I *had* to be going into something like a heat. Were his swamp monster pheromones transferring to me? Because I'd never felt this way before about a guy.

"Do you think your dad wants to swim?" I asked as we passed the closed front door of his lab building.

"He likes to go swimming, but he's working," Krill said. "And with snarly Baxi staying home, you and I can have some fun by ourselves."

"We *can* have fun, but I bet it would be entertaining with Baxi too."

"Only if you're into her snarling all the time."

Nope. I rested my hand on his shoulder, and despite him being only eight, he was already taller than me. Baxi towered over me as well, taking after her very tall father. Although, their mom could've been tall too.

We took a trail on the opposite side of the island that wove through denser woods. The trees here weren't quite as straggly, and the swamp had given way to mossy ground and then full-on grass. Frogs croaked in the distance, and a squirrel chittered at us from the canopy above. A light breeze played with the few strands of hair that had escaped my braid, and I decided there couldn't be a better day than today.

The sun was sending us a full-on blaze, and the day was getting humid already.

"Swimming is going to feel amazing," I said, curious to see what this swimming hole looked like.

Krill pointed ahead. "It's right there."

Blue water glistened, and we picked up our pace, exiting the trail out into the sunshine. I paused on the grassy bank of a large, spring fed pool, taking in the falls trickling down a series of boulders to our right and the overflow leaving the pool on our left.

"Did you dig this out?" I asked.

Krill shrugged. "It's always been here."

He dropped his bag and leaped into the water, making a big splash.

I should've asked if he could swim well, but when his head popped above the surface and he shot me a grin, my worry eased. He was a swamp kid. He'd probably been swimming here since he was born.

"Aren't you coming in?" he asked, pushing his palm across the surface, sending water my way. "It feels great."

I tugged off my sundress and dropped it on my bag with a towel. After ditching my flipflops, I walked down into the water at a more leisurely pace than him, gulping and gasping at how cold it felt. It had to be eighty out, yet the water felt about forty.

Eventually, I got brave and dove into the water, coming up sputtering. "It feels amazing!"

"Wonderful, huh?"

Like he was a seal, Krill ducked under and almost flew across the bottom of the pool. When he didn't come up for longer than I liked, my pulse jumped, and I sunk down, opening my eyes underwater to look for him.

He swam up behind me and tapped my spine. Nearly inhaling, I spun around and shook my head, bobbing back above the surface.

He popped up, grinning, his thick bands of hair draping across his face. He lifted his hand, revealing webbing between his fingers. "You don't need to worry about me. I'm kind of like a fish."

"I don't remember seeing webbing between your fingers, just your toes," I said.

"Finger webbing comes out when I swim. These too." He tapped his neck.

"You can breathe under water. Gills? Wow."

He nodded. "I could stay down for hours if I wanted to, but I wouldn't want to scare you."

"I appreciate that." I chuckled. "And here I was worried you could be drowning."

"I don't think I can." His gaze met mine. "Didn't you know? Swamp people are amazing."

He was totally right.

CHAPTER 16
THUL

I made myself remain in my lab, cataloging the new species I'd discovered in the swamp over the past week. Eventually, I'd publish my findings.

Instead of examining beetle wings beneath my microscope, I wanted to sit in the kitchen and stare at Amina. I wanted to eat her cookies. Talk to her about anything and everything.

I wanted to kiss her. Just the thought of claiming her mouth with my own made my lecturs spasm beneath my skin. Hormones flooded my veins, and my cock kicked into high gear. The lecturs buried within my cock twisted, and I nearly came in my pants at the thought of planting seed pods deep within her womb.

Groaning, I swiped my palms across my face.

I made myself get back to work, taking notes of my observations. I planned to test the solution this new species of beetle secreted to see what properties it held. Every now and then, a simple creature in nature could provide something that led to a cure for a disease or a medication that could alleviate symptoms. Other times, nothing came from a new discovery. But that was the wonder and beauty of this job. I never knew what I'd learn next about the world around me.

Amina's hair was soft and silky. I wanted to bury my face in it while I rocked myself inside her. It wasn't made up of thick bands like a swamp person's, and the color, while not unusual for a human, kept drawing my attention. I wanted to tuck my face into her nape and close my eyes while I ran my fingertips across her delicate shoulders. See if I could make her come from tugging on her nipples.

"Stop it," I barked to myself, focusing on the slide I was examining. "You need to be working, not daydreaming about your full mate and all you'd like to do with her."

After cataloguing the slide, I swiped secretions off the beetle and placed a sample of the liquid on slides. As I added various solutions to test the secretions' properties, I couldn't stop thinking about Amina's lovely eyes or her laugh when we worked on a puzzle, and I tried to fit a piece where it didn't belong. The way she looked at me when she didn't realize anyone was looking.

How wonderful my tail would feel buried inside her passage.

"Stop thinking about her tight, wet passage!"

I examined the beetle wing once more, noting a subtle pattern on the surface. Tugging my notebook closer, I drew a rough sketch of what I saw, doing my best to stop thinking about Amina. Things would work out as they should. My children were starting to like her —Krill, anyway. Baxi would take time, but I was sure she'd soon see how amazing Amina was.

What if she didn't? If I slept with Amina and we solidified our bond, I'd never be able to let her go. Actually, I was sure I wouldn't be able to let her go even if we didn't get together fully. She fit into my life seamlessly. I'd hate to think of a world where she wasn't a part of.

Why had the bureau decided my children would have the final say in whether we mated? That should be our decision, shouldn't it?

Growling, I stood and stalked across my lab, my cock a pole in my pants.

Outside, I stripped and raced across the small island. I wove around spindly trees and plunged into the swamp, sinking down until my belly rubbed across the mud coating the bottom.

I lay there for a bit before swimming deeper. Eventually, I reached the underworld where many of my people still lived. At the entrance, I coasted down the long tunnel, sliding along the mud coating the inner walls. I swam out into the clear pool, the foyer, so to speak, of this small village.

Cleansed of mud, I stalked up the shore, my gills flattening against my neck once more. I grabbed a cloth from the bin near the open doorway and secured it at my waist, shaking my head at the fact that we were now expected to cover our groins when we walked through the village. In the past, it didn't matter. It wasn't like anyone stared when someone strode about naked. But since we'd merged with the human world, however, we'd adopted some of their customs. Going clothed was just one of them.

And enjoying iced cream.

I waved to those I passed, smiling at their greetings. I hadn't been here in a very long time, and it was clear many had missed me. That warmed my heart and made me feel torn. I'd grown up here; enjoyed my life here. I was expected to rule here one day.

My first mate hadn't wanted to leave. But I wasn't drawn to rule, so I abdicated that right to the council. They did a much better job than I'd ever do.

To do credit to my research, I needed to live on the surface. I'd adjusted, though I wasn't sure Sharah ever had.

I strode down the path weaving among swamp monster homes, stopping at the healer's on the right. As I already knew, she was away for a few days, but her assistant was working, and he said he'd have the healer send a good supply of peristyle tea to my home when she returned.

Leaving, I continued down the path.

At the end of the trail, I ascended the stone steps leading to our central government building. Inside, I hurried to Agent Barclest's office, finding her seated on a moss pad with a great view of the village out her window opening.

"Dr. Hawkland," she said, rising.

I bowed as was customary, and she did the same.

"I've come to discuss my mating with the woman, Amina."

"Do you wish to end it already?"

"The opposite. She's my full mate." I lifted my arms, but my lecturs wouldn't respond to this female. only Amina. "I believe this fact should change the conditions."

One side of her brow ridge lifted. "Do you speak of any particular condition?"

"All of them, actually."

She sighed and waved to the large rock opposite her low stone desk. "Sit. Let's discuss this."

I settled, though I wanted this handled and to return home. Because I was so far from Amina, my body kept twitching. An overwhelming urge to be with her, touch her, and protect her kept roaring over me like a tidal wave. "She's my full mate. That should change the requirements. She shouldn't have to pass tests at all, and she should be accepted solely because she's triggered my mating heat."

"If anything, a full mating means she truly needs to pass all the tests."

"You'd discount her because she answered a question incorrectly?"

She shrugged. "Not one question. Our assumption is that humans will be nervous about mating with swamp monsters. We're not normal like gargoyles. We're more than ready to be generous with them, however. Five or six questions answered incorrectly might make us recon-sider, but it's not our goal to break up budding relationships. Please know we're not evil. We at the bureau want you and Amina to succeed."

"I'm worried. What if we decide we want to be together, but the bureau insists she must leave the island?"

"Monsters have settled predominantly on this island in this new home we constructed beneath the swamp, but you must know that we welcome humans. None have asked to settle here, but we'd greet them with open arms. Our species is slowly dying. Fewer young are born all the time, though you and your prior mate are to be commended for producing two tads."

I nodded slowly, not wanting to point out that a full mating almost guaranteed more tad implants solely due to the hormones charging through my body. Amina may not want to have many young, though she seemed open to the idea of at least one.

"Amina has done well so far," Agent Barclest said. "She passed the first test. She's basically halfway through the process. Won't you consider letting this play out as the bureau wants? There's only one more test, and then the interview with your young." She flashed her fangs my way. "I'm sure Baxi's and Krill's approval is merely a formality. They must be excited at the idea of having a new mother."

"Baxi's . . ." I wouldn't tip the agent off to the fact that my daughter could prove to be a problem.

"A delightful young swamp lady." She beamed. "I'm sure you're thrilled to have such a wonderful child in your home, as is Amina. Have they given each other mud facials or painted each other's skin with duloppir yet? My mother and I would collect the duloppir blossoms together and create the dye, then take turns painting patterns on each other's arms and shoulders. My father in particular adored it when I created intricate scenes on my mother's face. The dye would last for weeks!"

"They . . . haven't done either of those things yet."

Her smile remained true, and the softening of her eyes told me she was still reminiscing. "I'm sure they will."

"Yes, eventually." It was all I could do to maintain my neutral expression.

"Then everything will be fine. There's no need to worry, correct?" She rose. "I'd love to talk further, but I've got a meeting in a few moments. Do stop back again to chat if you're in the swamp village. It's always a joy to see you, Thul, and to hear about your latest research project."

"I will." Turning, I trudged toward the door. I wasn't going to get her to sign off on this, obviously. We'd have to make sure Amina was ready for the test and that Baxi voiced approval—something that seemed like an insurmountable hurdle.

"You can expect my next visit within a few days," the agent said. "We like to stay on top of arrangements like yours and Amina's. I'm sure she'll breeze right through the next questionnaire and after that, I'll be happy to speak with your young."

"Exactly when can we expect you to arrive?"

"Why not in three days?"

"So soon?"

That might not be enough time to work on Baxi.

"Is there a problem?" she asked, her brow tightening. "Since you've pointed out you're full mates, and she's triggered your mating heat, I assume you and Amina feel ready to take this to the final step."

"Not at all! That'll work well for us."

"Excellent. We can get this expedited, and then you and your full mate can disappear into the swamp for a bit." Her low laugh rang out. "I'm sure you're eager to plant some tads in her welcoming body."

"Oh, yes, I am." Of that, I was completely sure.

"Then I'll see you soon!" She flipped her hands my way, urging me from the office. I passed an elder swamp monster, one of the council, in the hall, and he bowed deeply.

"Meetra Thul," he rumbled. "So nice to see you."

I returned his bow. "You as well, Zuraton."

He entered the agent's office, shutting the panel behind him.

I walked back through the village, stopping to chat with one person after another. I'd have to come visit for a longer time soon. Perhaps Amina would like to come with me. We could ask one of my gargoyle friends to watch my young, and we could come to the village for the night. Perhaps at the next Critarek celebration. She'd love sampling all the food and dancing in the mud.

Rather than return to my lab, I decided to visit the swimming hole and wash off the purifying mud of the swamp. Most of the time, we left it on our skin until it dried and caked off. The healing properties within the swamp would sink into our flesh and we'd not only feel invigorated for days, but we'd also sleep better for weeks.

Laughter and excited cries made me pick up my pace as I approached the swimming hole. I was naked, but that was the norm. Who'd dress in human clothing while covered with mud?

Although . . . Amina wasn't swamp.

I paused while hidden in the woods. Perhaps I should enter the water downstream and wash off the mud before joining them.

My attention was caught by Amina emerging from the water wearing almost nothing. Humans covered their bodies all the time, but I'd never seen any of them wearing so little. Rather than mask her beauty, the skin-tight, two-piece outfit she wore only made her look more lush and lovely. Who would've thought that covering breasts and the juncture between a female's thighs could make her incredibly alluring?

My lecturs undulated beneath my skin, and I wasn't surprised to see them snap out from the tips of my fingers. They wove together and snaked through the woods.

Amina started to climb the tree with the rope I'd suspended for my young to swing out over the pool before letting go.

I couldn't see Krill, but I could hear him playing in the water upstream, squealing about how he was going to dive down and swim over to grab Amina when she dropped from the tree.

My lecturs found her.

They wrapped around her waist and tugged her toward me. At the same time, they pulled me from the woods and over to her.

She whirled around and gaped at my mud-covered form. "Thul." Her voice came out breathy, though it didn't appear she'd been running.

"Amina," I growled.

Her gaze fell to my stiff cock bobbing against my belly and remained there. The surprise in her face gave way to full-on desire.

The grin she gave me made the lecturs inside my cock start spinning.

"Well, well, well," she said. "You look happy to see me, Thul."

CHAPTER 17
AMINA

Thul was covered with mud.

He had a stiffy that rivaled an overgrown zucchini.

And the lecturs extending from his fingers like spiced-up vines were not only tugging me closer to him, but they were also making me tingle where they touched my bare skin, like he'd laced them with chili peppers—in a good way.

Warmth pooled low in my belly, and while I could hear Krill upstream, I couldn't see him.

If I stripped fast, jumped, and wrapped myself around Thul, could we see what that amazing cock could do?

Wait. Lecturs. Tads. No herbal tea to prevent lots of half-swamp monster babies.

I wasn't opposed to babies, half-swamp thing or other-wise, but I wasn't quite ready to start carrying them now.

"Hold that pose," I said, putting my palms between us.

"Mine," he growled.

Truly, I could appreciate how his inner swamp monster appeared to be taking over, eager to claim me, but now wasn't the right time.

"Yours," I agreed.

He flashed his fangs and his lecturs tugged me over until we bumped together. He fell backward—on purpose, I didn't knock him down—and while his lecturs retracted back into his fingers, his arms took their place, holding me against his amazing cock.

When we hit the ground, he rolled, putting me beneath him. He latched onto my wrists and gripped them in one big hand, holding them above my head.

"Mine," he snarled. "Now. Mate."

He was going all primeval on me, and I couldn't be more turned on by the fact.

Lowering his head, he claimed my mouth while his free hand roamed my wet body barely covered by my two-piece suit.

He plucked at my nipple while his mouth left mine, kissing down my neck to the juncture with my shoulder. When he bit down with his fangs, it was just enough to pinch but not enough to hurt.

Pleasure blasted through me, and I whimpered, ripping at my bottoms, determined to tug them down and beg him to plant that big old cock deep inside me. Who cared about lecturs and seed pods? Who cared about multiple tads? As long as he pounded himself inside me, I'd welcome everything that came with it.

Frustrated that my swimsuit bottoms wouldn't slide down, I gave up and bucked my hips toward him, spreading my legs around his hips. I rubbed my suit-covered clit against his engorged cock. The end of his tail coiled around my ankles, keeping me pinned against his groin.

"Yes, mate," he growled against my skin. "Claim. Now."

Take me to the cock and bestow it upon me, oh swamp monster gods.

"Hey Amina," Krill called out, his voice shocking through me and waking me from the lust inspired by Thul. "Where are you? Weren't you going to climb the tree and swing out over the pool on the rope?"

Thul's head jerked up, and his eyes cleared. He blinked down at me through his glasses speckled with mud. "We're on the ground. I'm naked. You're not quite naked but everything inside me tells me you should be."

"And your son is about to find us."

"Shit."

"The interruption sucks." And there was nothing new about it. His kids were one cock block after another, and my sexual frustration was going to make me explode —and not in a good way.

"I'm sorry," he said.

"Amina?" Krill yelled.

"I'll be there in a second. I'm . . . chatting with your father," I said. "Stay where you are, and I'll swing out over the water and drop into it, okay? You can find me below the surface."

"Okay!"

"At least he won't walk up to me lying on top of you," Thul said with a low laugh. "Or see my hard-on."

"You'd shock the poor child."

He shrugged. "While we're not exhibitionists, sex is part of everyday life among swamp monsters."

"I'm not opposed to testing out public sex, but I'm not doing it when your children might see."

He stilled. "You want to have public sex?"

"I don't mean in the middle of the general store but maybe we could sneak away and, I don't know, do it in an elevator while it's climbing to the top floor."

"There are no elevators on the island."

"You know what I mean. The thrill of being discovered might make it fun."

"I'll happily grind away at you anywhere you'd like, public or not."

"Once we have the herbs."

"Definitely once we have the herbs."

I rubbed his arms and chuckled as the mud flaked off. "Where have you been? Swimming in the swamp?"

"Yup."

Like, mud wrestling with Thul naked could be fun even if we didn't lie in the muck.

"I want to get you dirty," he said thoughtfully. "Very dirty. I want to make you beg and plead with me to make you come, and then I'm going to do it. Multiple times, in fact. Then I'll alternate riding you soft and hard until you're pleading once more."

"You're making me swoon so much, I'm not going to be able to walk to the tree, let along hold on to the rope until I can reach the pool."

"That's the point."

"Amina?" Krill said. "Do you need help climbing the tree?"

"I need to go," I said.

"Sadly, yes." He unwound his tail from my ankles, releasing me, and that was a really neat trick I hoped he'd used again in the future. After levering himself up and off me, he tugged me from the ground. "Spider inspection time."

"Ugh, you had to bring that up."

He ran his hands down my body, pausing at my breasts and teasing between my thighs, the fiend. I was a panting wreck by the time he spun me around and ran his fingers along the backs of my legs.

"If you bend forward some more," he growled by my ear. "I'll make sure nothing crawled beneath this scrap of fabric you're wearing to cover parts I can't wait to explore."

"If you keep up the dirty talk, I'm going to come from that alone."

"Now that would be a shame. I want to suck on you and stroke everything before you finally give way."

I bent forward and wiggled my butt.

He ran his fingers across my ass and legs again and

dipped them beneath the fabric—though not far enough for me—before sighing. "No spiders."

I straightened and turned to face him. "You sound disappointed."

"Maybe they're hiding beneath your top. I could remove all it and make sure you're completely safe."

Safe and a few other things I'd love to explore, but nope. Not right now.

I shook my finger at him. "Behave. I have to return to your son and you, my fine swamp monster . . ."

His head tilted. "What would you have me do?"

Sauntering around him, I called over my shoulder. "Meet with me tonight at the swimming hole. It's time you put your words into action."

CHAPTER 18
THUL

All I wanted to do was climb a tree near the swimming hole and watch Amina as she played in the water. Talk about swamp stalking.

Instead, I made myself head downstream, where I washed off the mud. I returned to where I'd left my clothing and dressed, then made myself go to my lab.

I didn't leave until it was close to dinnertime, though I barely worked. I spent most of my time dreaming about how beautiful Amina was while wearing almost nothing, how eager I was to see her when she *was* wearing nothing, how much I adored her laugh, and how I ached to be with her fully.

My damn cock kept rising from my thoughts, and I finally gave up and closed my lab for the night.

As I approached my home, laughter rang out inside, Krill's high-pitched tone mingling with Amina's. I stopped and a grin stretched my lips so wide, it made my face hurt.

I loved this woman, and it was clear Krill would soon feel the same if he didn't already. Even my worry about what Baxi might tell the bureau didn't make my grin fade one bit.

My lecturs spiraled beneath my skin as I opened the door and stepped inside. Like always, I removed my shoes. I only wore them to placate humans. A swamp thing like me didn't need footwear. Clothing either, but I also donned that in case I had visitors.

Like Amina.

She'd admired my mud-covered body. She'd ground herself against my mud-covered cock.

There was nothing better than falling in love.

Amina and Krill sat at the counter working on a puzzle. I wanted to stride over and impress her with my ability to place the correct piece in the right spot but instead, I just watched, drinking in the sight of her playing with my son.

Amina smiled my way. "Dinner will be served in fifteen minutes. I hope you're hungry. We're having a mix of human and swamp thing specialties prepared by the best chefs in this house—me and Krill."

I sniffed the air, and my belly growled. "I can't wait."

Baxi sat in the recliner staring toward the kitchen with longing in her pretty eyes.

I stopped beside her and stooped down, keeping my voice low. "You know, you could join them at any time."

She crossed her arms over her chest, and her eyes shimmered with tears. "I don't know how."

"It's okay to have fun with Amina. I'd hate to see you wallowing in sadness forever."

Pinching her eyes shut, she sighed. "I miss Mom so much."

"We all do." Straightening, I rubbed her shoulders. "She was special. No one will ever take her place."

Opening her eyes, she looked up at me. "You mean that? Really?"

"Really. She'll always be your mom."

Baxi's eyes turned to her brother and Amina. "I suppose it wouldn't be so bad to help with the puzzle."

"Not bad at all. It would make Krill happy." Amina too, but I'd let Baxi discover that on her own.

"Maybe later." My heart sunk until she rose and walked over to the counter. "Want me to help you set the table for dinner?" she asked Amina.

Amina's breath caught, and her gaze darted to me before she smoothed her features. "That would be great, Baxi. Thank you."

"Yeah, so don't . . ." My daughter's voice cut off. She might still sound sullen, but I had hope that she was starting to soften to the idea of having Amina in our lives.

"What's on the menu tonight?" I asked eagerly. I adored just being with Amina. I didn't need anything else. But she was an amazing cook, and I couldn't wait to see what she'd serve next.

"Mac 'n cheese and lily pad wraps." She looked Baxi's way. "I know you prefer meat, so the wraps are stuffed with gator sausage, herbs, and tubers Krill and I dug near the swimming hole. Krill helped make everything, and I bet he'll grow up to be an amazing chef." Leaving the puzzle, she started bringing dishes of food over to the table, and we sat.

Krill blushed and scooped up a big serving of mac—whatever a mac was—and cheese, adding two of the wraps to his plate.

"I'm open to eating more than meat," Baxi said carefully, not looking Amina's way.

"Whatever you're comfortable with." Amina sent me a quick grin. "I'll be happy to prepare your favorite dishes if you tell me what they are."

"Not my favorites Mom used to make," she said.

"The only way we should serve those is if you make them for us." Amina swallowed hard, and her eyes shimmered with tears, but I knew they came from sympathy for my daughter; she wasn't upset.

Thank you, I mouthed, grateful once more that the bureau had matched me with this wonderful woman.

"Maybe I could make one of them sometime," Baxi said. "You might like them too." Her gaze darted to Amina's face before flicking away.

"I'm sure I will," Amina said softly.

This start gave me hope things would get better between them.

And tonight, I'd take the first step in claiming my mate.

I was voraciously hungry for Amina. Her touch. Her kiss. Her body pressed against mine.

And even more, for her love.

CHAPTER 19
AMINA

After cleaning up the dinner dishes, Krill and I finished the puzzle with Thul's help. Baxi joined us and placed a few pieces, though she pretended she only did it because her brother asked her. Still, it was a step in the right direction.

I wasn't sure when the bureau would ask Krill and Baxi if they wanted me in their lives, but I hoped Baxi had warmed enough by then that she'd say she liked me and thought I'd fit into their family. Krill would, and I wanted to kiss his cute little face whenever he smiled my way.

When the puzzle was finished, I got out the chocolate cake I'd made. "Anyone want some?"

"Yum," Krill said, wiggling on his stool. "Can I have a big piece? When it was cooking, it smelled so good, I wanted to yank it from the oven and eat it all up."

"One big slice coming up." I cut into the treat and placed a chunk on a plate I slid over to Krill. "Thul?"

"I'm always up for something tasty." The heat in his gaze told me exactly what he hoped to be tasting soon.

My pulse thudded fast in my ears, and heat kept swirling through me, centering in my clit.

I couldn't wait until the kids went to bed and we could sneak out to the pool.

Could my life get any better than this?

I cut Thul his cake and nudged my chin toward Baxi who still hung back but hadn't left to hide in her room. "Would you like some, Baxi?"

"Um, I *suppose* so," she said. "I'm not sure I like chocolate much, but you did put in a lot of effort, so I'll try it."

"I even made the frosting. It's chocolate buttercream and my own recipe."

"Totally yum," Krill said, his face smeared with chocolate. He gulped down the last bite from his plate and gazed longingly at the rest of the cake. "I don't suppose I could have more?"

"Tomorrow," Thul said. "One slice per day is enough."

"Ugh. Parental guidance is such a pain." With that, he slid off his stool, put his plate in the dishwasher, and started toward his room. "I'll be reading if you should need me."

"Don't forget to wash and do your fangs," I called out as he left.

"Yup, yup." He backtracked to scoop up a pile of books from the coffee table in the living room, and if I knew him, he'd be up for hours, reading.

It was summer, though, and he didn't have school. Let the kid enjoy staying up late. Reading had to be better than watching TV.

Baxi's eyes sparkled. "Even Mom had a hard time getting him to do his fangs." The humor left her gaze, but she remained with us at the island, carefully eating her slice of cake. When she was finished, she put her plate in the dishwasher. "Night." With that, she left, and I considered it a plus when she didn't slam her door.

Thul and I exchanged glances.

"She's warming up nicely," Thul said. "When you first got here, she wouldn't have touched the cake."

"When I first baked, she ate a bunch of cookies."

"They were excellent, that's why."

"Where does Krill get all his books?"

Thul finished his slice of cake and licked the plate. What a nice, long tongue he had . . .

Looking my way, his face darkened.

I lifted my plate and did the same thing.

His face darkened even more. Was he thinking of where our tongues might go in the future? I sure was.

"I take Krill to the library in town every other week." He took his plate to be washed. "At this rate, he's going to read everything they have there within a year. It's a decent-sized library, and they have a large kid's section, but he has a voracious appetite for books."

"Maybe we should get him an e-reader."

Turning, he leaned against the counter, his eyes lighting up. "I've heard of them. Could we put some parental controls on what he reads?"

"Yes, plus how much he's allowed to spend on books," I said with a laugh. "Or you'll get a big surprise when you see your credit card bill."

"I'm not worried about the money. Books are amazing. He can read as many as he'd like."

"I noticed he's reading a lot of fantasy and sci-fi."

"His favorite genres."

"I put a few of my favorite series in storage, but I can go to the mainland and pick them up. I imagine he'll love them as much as me."

"That's sweet of you."

I covered the cake, and we settled in the living room.

"How do you want to do this?" I asked softly, meaning sneaking out to the pool.

"Any way I can."

He sounded so earnest, my laugh snorted out. I leaned against his arm, liking how warm he was, how nice it was to snuggle against him. We definitely had chemistry, but being able to laugh with him, talk with him, made everything perfect. If Baxi continued to soften, I could see us making this work.

"I'll sneak out first and make sure we have nothing to worry about at the pool," he said.

"Slay my dragons, and I'll love you for life."

He peered down at me. "I'm there already. I need you to know that."

"Same." My voice came out a croak. "I need *you* to know that."

"Amina," he breathed, turning to hold my face. He kissed me much too quickly. I barely had time to let the swimming feeling sink into my bones before he lifted his head. "Soon."

His lecturs were churning beneath his skin again.

I slid my finger along one, and he released a shiver. "Sorry." I lifted my finger off his skin. "I didn't hurt you, did I?"

He took my hand and kissed my fingertip. "Only in one location."

I couldn't miss the bulge pressing against the front of his jeans. My pulse rocketed through my head, and I got suddenly breathless. Leaning toward him, I gave him a sultry smile. "Soon, we'll be able to take care of your—"

"Does Amina have something in her eye?" Baxi asked. She stopped behind the sofa, the beginning of her glare sweeping between us.

Yeah, she knew I didn't have anything in my eye.

"I'm fine," I said.

"Lightheaded, then? You're almost falling on Dad."

"Weren't you going to bed?" Thul asked.

Her lips twisted. "Eventually. I wanted a drink of water."

One side of his brow ridge lifted. "Then get one."

With a heavy sigh, she trudged into the kitchen, her tail whipping back and forth. She filled a glass and took it toward her room, not saying anything else to us.

Thul echoed her sigh once her door shut sharply behind her.

Two steps forward, one step back, but I was heading in the right direction. It just might take some time to get there.

We sat and stared at the blank TV, and I didn't really want to turn it on. As nice as it was to kiss Thul, I didn't mind the silence. It felt soothing.

"Twenty minutes more?" he finally whispered.

I nodded. "It'll be okay to leave them for a bit?"

"Of course. We won't go far."

Taking his hand, I linked our fingers. The bands of collapsed webbing on the sides of his tickled and felt odd, but good. I liked our differences. They made us unique.

He lifted my hand and kissed my knuckles. Such a simple gesture, yet it sparked a need deep inside me, one I suspected only this guy would ever satisfy. I'd been with others, but none had touched me in the same way as Thul.

Standing, he gave me a smile that melted my bones. "I'll go make sure it's safe. Join me soon?"

I sucked in a breath and nodded, watching as he strode toward the front door.

"No swimsuit?" I asked as he reached for the knob.

He winked. "I don't need one."

Because I couldn't help but worry about leaving them even if only for a short while, I knocked on each of the kids' doors and told them I was going to take a walk. Baxi huffed and said nothing. Krill told me to have a wonderful time, then ducked his nose back into his book.

After changing into a sundress—no suit for me tonight either—and grabbing a towel, I scuffed my feet into my flipflops and grabbed a flashlight from the hook on the kitchen wall. By shining the light on the path outside and watching where I placed my feet, I was able to ignore the splashes and scurrying sounds coming from either side as I hurried through the swamp. My breath whooshed out of me when I reached the island with Thul's lab.

Hurrying past the building, I entered the trail leading to the pool. Moonlight filtered through the canopy and while I could turn off my flashlight, I felt more comfortable seeing where I stepped. That would teach me to wear high-top boots instead of sandals.

I reached the pool and turned off the light, letting my eyes adjust to the darkness. Not seeing Thul, I watched the water and surrounding area for a while, making sure no creatures had decided it was a great time to swim. Seeing and hearing nothing unusual, I dropped my towel and lifted my sundress up over my head. My underwear soon followed, and my bare skin quivered in anticipation.

Thul would be here soon. Maybe he swam upstream or stopped at his lab to check on something.

I would wait for him in the pool.

I walked down the bank and into the water, trying not to cringe at how cold it was. It would feel wonderful once I was wet and moving around, and even better once Thul joined me.

Soon, I was submerged and floating. I dipped down to wet my hair and treaded water, gazing up at the moon, grinning. My skin no longer quivered at the temperature. See? Perfect.

Splashes erupted behind me. I spun to find someone's head jutting up from the water. Moonlight glinted on his fangs.

Thul's smile widened. "Did you know that swamp creatures can see as well in the dark as in the light?"

CHAPTER 20
THUL

After making sure there were no threats in or near the water, I sunk down to the bottom of the pool and lounged.

I had a great view of my lovely mate gingerly walking into the water.

"There you are." Her teeth flashed white in the dark. "I thought you might still be in the lab."

I floated closer. "The lab has nothing on you, Amina."

"Can you really see just as well in the dark as in the light?"

"Yup. You're beautiful. Perfect. I'm not sure I deserve you."

She placed her palms on my shoulders. "Maybe I'm the one who doesn't deserve *you*."

"Or we *do* deserve each other."

"I prefer that." She tipped her head back, wetting her hair, then sent me a shy look. "The water feels amazing."

"It's wet. Cool."

Her fingers tightened on my skin. "What do you want to do now that we've snuck away from the children to finally be alone together in this cool wetness?"

"Talk?"

Her laugh trilled across the water. "Yes, do tell me. What's your favorite color?"

He lifted his arm. "Green like my skin."

"I'm partial to green too."

His fangs flashed whitely. "What's your favorite season?"

"Spring."

"The season of hope."

"I love summer but once summer's gone, it's fall."

"Fall's nice. Crackling leaves, the smell of woodsmoke from fires in the air. The air's crisp and cool."

"But you see, fall leads into winter and it's cold."

"That's where those fires come in."

"I adore the warmth, which is why I like spring the most. It's warming up to the heat I savor."

"Then you actually love summer the most."

I grinned. "Didn't I say that?"

"I suppose you did." He chuckled, his fingers trailing up and down my spine. It was easy to get lost in his touch, in the sensations he created inside me.

"What's *your* favorite season?"

"Whichever one you're in with me."

"You say the right things all the time."

"Because they come from my heart." My voice came out raspy.

"No, really."

"It's fall because it gives me a feeling of completion, like the world's about to reset itself with winter. Spring's full of hope and the feeling of being renewed, but I like wrapping things up before starting something new."

"That's the scientist in you."

"Yup." I couldn't believe she was here with me, finally. And we wore nothing. Yet we talked about seasons. I liked that we could do something like this, but she was right that we probably shouldn't leave my young alone for too long.

"We're in the spring of our relationship, starting something new with lots of promise."

"I'm so grateful I met you."

"Now I'm here. We're finally alone."

"Hopefully for more than two minutes," I said with a laugh.

"I think we have time to explore whatever we choose."

"Does that mean you want to look for creatures?" I said with a laugh.

A shiver tracked through her, and I tugged her against my body. Suddenly, I wasn't thinking about pool exploration, the seasons, or whether or not we'd be alone for long. All I could think of was her.

My lecturs started spiraling up and down my arms, and the ones in my cock twisted so tight, it was almost painful.

I kissed her, savoring the way she pressed herself against me, the way her fingers clutched my shoulders, and the way she made me feel as if nothing and no one was more important than us and this moment.

I slid my tail around her waist, tugging her even closer.

When I lifted my head, she gave me the sexiest smile. It made my lectures glide from my fingertips. They coiled around her and stroked her back.

Kissing her again, I retracted my finger lectures so I could touch her breasts, savoring how lush they were, how much I ached to taste them.

Why not now?

I slid down into the water, seamlessly breathing with my gills, and sucked on one breast while stroking the other. She arched her spine, thrusting her breast into my mouth, and even through the water, I could hear her heady moans.

She was the light I'd forever seek in darkness and the heat that would warm my cold heart. My life would be empty without her.

I nudged her thighs apart with my knee and teased my tail down across her belly. Pausing with the thick tip at the juncture between her thighs, I sought approval for what I'd like to do to her, with her.

Realizing she might not know what I was asking, I bobbed above the surface. "What do you think about tails?"

"I like your tail," she said with a sultry smile. "Though I don't think you're looking for a general opinion."

"It's like an arm or a leg to me, and the tip is as sensitive as fingers."

She shivered, and her eyes darkened. "What would you like to do with your tail?"

"I can't fuck you with my cock like I ache to do, not until we have the herb, or both want tads."

"I can wait for the herbs."

I wasn't sure I could, but I'd find a way. "Let me pleasure you with my tail, my mouth, and my fingers."

She stroked my face. "You mean so much to me. I'm not sure there are enough words to describe the feelings I have for you. So, yes. Please. I want to be with you in any way I can."

I kissed her again, loving the way she clung to me, the way she bucked her body against mine.

I released the lecturs from my fingers again, guiding some to her breasts and the others between her legs, finding her clit.

She moaned and tipped her head back, closing her eyes, and I supported her with my arms while using my lecturs and tail to give her pleasure. As I rubbed her clit, she rocked against it.

Electric jolts shot from the tip of my tail and finger lecturs, and my cock rose in response. Touching her like this gave me almost the same pleasure as if I'd buried my shaft inside her. I'd come just from touching her this way alone.

Sinking down beneath the water again, I spread her legs, placing her thighs on my shoulders. She held onto the top of my head while I stroked across her entrance with my tongue. Soon, I couldn't resist the guttural sounds of excitement she made, and I plunged my tongue deep inside her. I stroked her inner walls, flicking the split tip high inside to give her more pleasure.

She rode my mouth and lecturs, but that still wasn't enough. I stroked my tail down between her legs and nudged the thick tip into her entrance. When she stilled, so did I.

But she stroked my hair and urged me on with her soft cries, so I drove my tail deep within her.

Heat flared in my cock, and the inner lecturs tightened.

Just feeling my tail move within her heated me to a boiling point. My cock secreted lubricant and thrust hard against my abs. What I wouldn't give to bury it deep inside her. I'd ride her until she cried out my name, then start over and take her there once more.

While she gasped and jerked toward me, I stroked her inner walls with my tongue, coiling it around my tail that moved slowly at first, then faster at her urging. Each thrust ricocheted to my cock, and it grew even stiffer.

The inner lecturs coiled tight, then released and slid up toward the tip.

"More," she moaned, rocking against my mouth and tail. "It's . . ." Her words dissolved in a groan.

She started shuddering around me and barked out a cry that sunk into my soul like the most precious treasure in the world.

I came along with her, my lecturs erupting from the

tip of my cock, twisting and fluttering while shooting seed pods into the water.

One day, I'd plant them within her, but for now, this was more than enough.

When Amina's body loosened, and she stopped snarling her fingers through my hair, I rose back to the surface.

We kissed, and she stroked my face.

Then I held her, floating on my back while she lay across my chest.

CHAPTER 21
AMINA

I'd never experienced anything like this, and I knew I never would again, other than with Thul.

"I don't believe I've had an orgasm that good in my life." I didn't feel vulnerable for sharing how wonderful that had been, nor how much I'd come to love him. No matter what happened with the bureau, we had this.

"Me either."

"I'm glad you're not in pain."

"Never." His arms tightened around me. "Even if I didn't come, I'd feel just as happy. You . . ." His voice deepened. "You're amazing. I've been with others, as you know. But what you and I have found together is special. I don't want to go back to the person I was before I met you."

I turned to face him, still lying across his chest while he held me afloat. Our legs entwined, linking us in a way that felt precious. "I love everything about you."

His eyes, so dark and full of affection, met mine. "I'm

in love with you, Amina. That's not going away. I'm not going away. Never. Well, I suppose if you kick me out—"

"It's your house."

"Ours. You're my mate, the only woman I'm ever going to love, and everything I have is yours. My possessions. My heart. My soul."

"I can't imagine my life without you, Thul." I didn't want to jinx things by bringing up the tests I still had to pass, the feeling that there wasn't much I could do to make Baxi like me. I wouldn't give up until all hope was lost, and we weren't anywhere near that point in our lives.

He cupped my cheeks tenderly and curled up to kiss me. It didn't take anything more than that to spark my body once more, and I was soon rocking against his engorged cock, wishing we could take this in whatever direction we pleased.

Riding him still felt good, and his ragged breathing told me he was enjoying the friction as much as me.

His tail stroked my inner thighs in a way that tickled but fed my inner fire. And when his lecturs spiraled out of his fingers, some coiling around my nipples to tug on them, others finding my clit, I cried out in joy. I'd just had a fantastic orgasm. How could I want more?

Because I was with him. I was going to crave this guy for the rest of my days, and I'd finally accepted that fact.

As the tip of his tail glided higher and higher on my thighs, I spread my legs. And when he plunged it inside me, I barked out a shriek that echoed around us.

I rode his tail while it moved inside me, his lecturs driving me to a fever peak on my breasts and clit.

I still found a way to move against his cock. There was no way I was leaving him behind. The tip kept gliding through my folds, releasing a lubricant that didn't dissolve in the water. The liquid slid inside me, making the movement of his tail even smoother.

I was going to explode, and we'd barely gotten started.

Arching my spine, I groaned with each thrust.

And when I came, he growled. His cock spasmed, and he cupped my face, keeping our eyes locked together until I collapsed onto his chest once more.

As we slowly walked back to the house, my legs flopped around like rubber. I'd had three orgasms in the pool courtesy of Thul, and he'd joined me in each one.

I couldn't wait to go swimming again.

He held my hand, and he kept stopping me on the path, lifting me with his tail to kiss me. When he pressed me against the outer wall of his lab, I spread my legs around him and ground against his cock that had risen once more.

"I'm your sex slave," I admitted with a grin once he'd lifted his head to stare down at me.

"Tell me what you want. What you need, and I'll give it to you. Anything. Me? I'm already yours. My heart? Ditto. My soul succumbed the moment I met you."

He couldn't grant me what I wanted, so I wouldn't

name it. That was up to the bureau, but surely, they'd be able to see how deeply we loved each other. They wouldn't drive us apart, would they?

"You're all I need, Thul. Just you."

He kissed me so sweetly that it brought tears to my eyes. When he lifted his head, I read the deep love he had for me there.

"I'll keep working on Baxi," I said. She was so easy to love. I could only hope she'd soon decide I could be a friend. I'd never try to step into her mom's place. That was a precious spot that didn't need to belong to me. But she must have room in her heart for someone new.

"I can talk with her," he said.

I shook my head. "Don't. We can't force it. I don't want to, and it wouldn't be right. We'll give her the time she needs."

He sighed. "I swam to the village I grew up in deep beneath the swamp and spoke with Agent Barclest today. She'll come by in three days to administer the second test."

"I think I'll do okay, right? I did well enough with the first. I'll speak from my heart, and she'll see we deserve to be together."

"You'll do well. I know it." He rubbed his palms up and down my arms, creating a warm friction that sunk into my bones. Like every other time he touched me, his lecturs rippled beneath his skin, and my body responded, going from a simmer to a full boil.

"Thanks." I gave him a shy smile. "Soon, the tests will be behind us, and we can be together forever."

"Exactly."

I sucked in a breath and released it. "As for Baxi's and Krill's approval, I'm sure the agent will give me time to work with them before she asks for their input."

He pinched his eyes shut and opened them. "That's the thing . . ."

Concerned spiraled inside me, coiling into a tight ball that made my belly sink. "Did she mention a date?"

"The same day as your second test. She's going to speak with them three days from now."

CHAPTER 22

THUL

"That's not enough time," Amina said, her eyes shimmering with tears. "Baxi will tell the agent she hates me, and I'll be forced to leave."

"I'm sorry." I hated seeing her upset. It brought out all my protective instincts. My lecturs thrashed beneath my skin, some shooting out from my fingers, forming blades. Long ago, agitation like this would turn my regular old swamp monster body into a weapon I'd use to defend my mate and young.

Instead, one of my young was going to use a weapon against me and Amina.

Amina shook her head. "No, it will be enough time. I'll try harder. There must be a way to reach her." Her smile came out shaky. "Three days can make a huge difference."

If Baxi ruined this for us, I'll appeal to the council. Amina and I were full mates. That had to count for something.

I kissed her, hoping to lend her my strength, but her hand shook in mine as we walked back to the house together. Inside, we were greeted with silence. We checked on Baxi and Krill, finding them both asleep, Krill still holding a book in his hand as he slumped sideways on his pillow.

Amina gently took it from him, placed the bookmark where he'd left off and laid it on the bedside table. She stroked his hair off his face and sent me such a loving smile, it made my heart shatter.

She was the best thing that could've happened to me and my family, and I wasn't going to give her up. I'd fight to be with her, and I'd use any weapon I could lay my hands on.

In Baxi's room, Amina stood beside the bed staring down at my daughter with a longing on her face that crushed whatever was left of my heart after it was shattered by how kindly she'd treated my son.

She carefully tugged the blanket up over my daughter's shoulders and ran the back of her knuckle down Baxi's cheek.

We left the room, shutting the door behind us, and walked to our hallway where we paused outside Amina's door. I wanted to invite her into my bed, but I also wanted to be careful with my young. Amina was new to our family, and while Krill was all-in, I wanted to respect Baxi's feelings even if I had no interest in catering to them.

"I'll see you in the morning?" I said, fingering

Amina's oh-so-soft hair. I could touch it all day. Bury my face in it all night.

She bit down on her lower lip, then gave me a shaky smile. "I'll make something new for breakfast."

"I appreciate you so much. Not just because you're perfect for my family, but because you're the best person for me. That's not going to change, no matter what. No one's going to drive a wedge between us. Will you trust me to make sure this comes out right?"

"We won't let anyone tear us apart," she said, but her voice came out bleak. She wasn't giving up, that wasn't Amina. But I could tell her confidence was shaken by the rushed deadline.

I kissed her deeply, wishing I could love her once more, but we had tomorrow, the day after that, then all the days of our lives to be together.

I lowered her back to the floor with my tail, and she went inside her room.

I walked to my own room and went inside, quickly undressing and doing my fangs in my adjoining bathroom. Lying in my bed after, I tossed and turned.

Should I speak to the council about a delay? The thought made me feel even more unsettled. Because relationships like mine and Amina's were new, the council was also watching us closely. Asking for more time might make them balk since they weren't eager for any of us to consider a relationship with a human at all.

A full mating with Amina should make a difference, but I wasn't sure I trusted them enough to ask them to intervene.

No, I'd wait. If something went horribly wrong, then I'd speak up.

While I might not feel the need—yet—to speak to the council, I needed to have a conversation with Baxi. Nothing was going to hold me back. I loved my new mate, and I wanted to be with her. While I hoped Baxi would one day care for Amina as much as me, we didn't have months or a year for her to warm up to the idea that Amina was going to be her stepmom.

"Do you have a moment?" The next day, I stood in Baxi's open doorway. Finding it open was encouraging since I could hear Amina and Krill playing a game at the island in the kitchen from here. Not long ago, Baxi would've shut the door to block out the sound of them having fun.

Her face became guarded. "I suppose so." She'd been laying on her bed, staring at her phone, but she swung her legs around to sit and tossed the phone onto the bed beside her.

After closing the door, I crossed the room, moved the phone to her bedside table, and took its place.

"I assume you're here to tell me I need to be nicer to Amina." Her arms were crossed on her chest, her tail looped around her waist protectively. "If so, you can leave. I'm trying, and that's all I'm going to promise."

"I see." I said nothing, thinking about a new strategy, because she'd stolen the words from my mouth. "We all miss your mom."

"I do. I'm less sure about Krill, and as for you, I believe you've moved on."

"She died."

She reeled away from me. "As if I don't know that?"

"It's been two years."

"It feels like yesterday to me." Tears sprung up in her eyes. "I think about her all the time. Miss her all the time. But not you. You interred her ashes in the swamp with our ancestors and jumped into a bizarre relationship with a human."

"Why is it bizarre to have a relationship with a human?"

"She's not like us. She doesn't understand our culture or anything about how we live."

"We'll teach her. She's eager to learn."

"She's just pretending."

I shook my head. "That's not true. She's trying. Harder than you, I'll add."

"I don't want to like her."

Now here was something I could work with. "Why not? Not enough room in your heart to care about more than me, Krill, and your mom?"

"I'm not stupid. I know you're going to say that we have the capacity to love many people in our lives."

"Because it's true."

"I'm more than happy to love others, but that doesn't mean I want to live with them."

"Where would you have her live?"

"She could try out the swamp since she's so eager to understand our culture."

"Don't be mean. She's not built to survive something like that."

"She has no gills or webbing. No tail. No fangs. She's completely useless. She jumps when a fly goes near her face, and I'm sure she'll scream if a mosquito bites her."

"Now you're being sarcastic."

"Even ignoring all that, she'll never be a full part of our lives."

"You're saying you'd be okay with me having a relationship with another swamp monster." I hated naming it. How had I raised a child who couldn't see beyond her own species?

"That's *not* what I'm saying."

"It sounds like it to me." I stood. This conversation only seemed to be making her angrier, not building bridges she wasn't willing to cross.

"I don't want her here." She latched onto my arm. "Please, Dad. Make her leave."

"No."

Her face cratered, but she didn't cry.

I strode to the door but turned back before opening it. "I like Amina. No, I'm in love with her. I was a good mate to your mom. I've mourned her loss. But that doesn't mean I don't deserve to be happy with someone new."

CHAPTER 23
AMINA

I didn't miss Thul going to Baxi's room, nor her slamming her bedroom door behind him when he left.

He walked past me with deadened steps, leaving the house.

"Go after him," Krill said softly. "I'll go speak with my sister." He slid off his stool and scooted down the hall, where he knocked on Baxi's door.

I left the house and took the trail around it and across to the island with his lab. Sensing he wasn't there, I kept going. I found him sitting on the bank of the pool where we'd had so much fun the night before.

"Is it okay for me to join you?" I asked. Maybe he wanted to be alone.

He reached up, took my hand, and tugged me down onto his lap, where he held me, his chin on the top of my head while he stared at the water.

"It's tough being a parent sometimes," I said, though it wasn't like I had any experience.

"Yeah."

"She's a good kid."

"Sometimes. Other times, she's a pain in the tail."

My lips twitched upward, but I didn't smile. "I assume you spoke to her about me."

"Unfortunately, my daughter would like me to spend the rest of my life mourning her mother."

"That's not unusual."

"Did you snap and snarl at your stepfather?"

"I had my moments, though not often. But my mom didn't meet him until a long time after my dad's death. It's tough losing a mom. I think about mine all the time. I miss her, and not just being around her. We did a lot of things together. We were best friends. You just can't shut that off because the person's no longer there. The end was torture for us both. The disease went to her mind, and most of the time, she didn't even know who I was."

"I'm sorry."

"No, I'm the one who's sorry. I came after you to give you a chance to talk and vent, but I'm sharing about myself instead of listening."

"It's all right. It's natural to equate yourself with Baxi. You're both daughters who lost mothers too soon."

"She's a child still, though. Twelve is on the cusp of being a grown up while still being a kid. I'm sure she feels mature enough to control her own life, because I felt that way when I was twelve. But that's why we're here to protect her. Guide her."

"She doesn't want my guidance. She wants to lament about what she lost without realizing that we can move forward and still bring memories of her mom along with us."

"It takes more maturity than a twelve-year-old possesses to realize something like that. She needs more time." Which we didn't truly have. The day after tomorrow was rushing up to us, and whatever she told Agent Barclest would have a profound impact on all our lives.

"I'm grateful to have you for many reasons, Amina. I love how thoughtful you are with me, how kind. I adore how you've made friends with Krill. And seeing you keep trying with Baxi despite how she behaves makes me love you even more."

I turned in his arms, wrapping my legs and arms around him, giving him as big a hug as I could. "I'm sorry," I mumbled against his chest. "You deserve the world. No one should hold you back."

"Thanks."

"I'll continue to bake goodies to introduce her to the side of humans she seems to enjoy—our food. I'll urge her to hang out with me and Krill, play games, do puzzles, and everything else. I'm not going to exclude her, though I would never force her to do something with us. But if I'm there, always cheerful and open, she's bound to start realizing I'm not a threat."

He sighed. "What if she never lets down her guard?"

"Never?" I gasped, shooting him a smile. "I dare her to try."

He rubbed my back, and we snuggled a bit before we got up and walked back toward the house. There was no fixing this, and rehashing it wasn't doing either of us any good.

At his lab, he stopped. "I've got some stuff to take care of here."

"You go do your thing." I peered toward the house. "I'll go do my part with the kids."

He kissed me, his lips lingering on mine. "You're amazing." He stroked my hair and stared into my eyes, his tail coiling around my waist.

"You're amazing yourself," I said, breathless after our kiss.

"I'll see you soon?"

I nodded and stood there, watching until he'd entered his lab and shut the door. Then I made my over-heated body take me back to the house. I found Krill sitting in a chair, reading. Baxi sat on the sofa. She took one look at me and started to rise.

Krill cleared his throat, and she shot him a glare and sat back down. Coercion? I wouldn't put it past the eight-year-old going on seventy, but I wasn't sure I wanted her to pretend. At least her glare put things out into the open, and the snide way she ran her gaze down my body made it clear that if I'd made any strides forward, I'd slide back to the starting point with her.

Actually, that wasn't true. We'd talked, she'd eaten the food I'd prepared, and she'd stood at the island the night before, helping me and Krill put together a puzzle.

So she'd taken a step away from me again. I'd keep

being myself, and she'd see it was safe to interact with me. Maybe she'd even one day see me as a friend.

We had lunch, Baxi volunteering to bring her father his share when he sent word that he was busy and wouldn't be able to join us.

Krill and I spent the afternoon swimming in the pool with Baxi sitting on the shore sending me glares.

Krill swam over close to her and sent a burst of water her way with his tail.

"Don't be such a baby." She rose to her feet, backing away. Her tail coiled around her waist, and she blinked fast.

"You're the one who's being a baby," Krill said. "A mean old baby who should just stay in the house if you're going to be cranky."

She looked at him like he'd totally betrayed her, and maybe, in her eyes, he had. Whirling around, she raced back to the house.

"Maybe be a little more patient with her," I said. "She's having a hard time."

He swam back to the middle of the pool, joining me. "She's giving *you* a hard time, and I don't like it. I get it. I miss Mom too. But you're not Mom. You're a separate person, and you're living with us now. I like you, and I don't want her being such a pisser to you."

"I appreciate you defending me, but maybe just ignore how she's acting?"

He huffed. "Ignoring it doesn't seem to be making it go away, does it?"

"It's getting better."

One side of his brow ridge lifted. "That, I'm not seeing." He dipped down into the pool, sinking to the bottom, where he remained for longer than I liked, but he had gills. While he could drown, I doubted he would. Finally, he bobbed up and gave me a grin that told me he knew I'd been worried.

I ruffled his hair. "You. Don't do that again without . . ."

"What? Telling you I'm going to float on the bottom for a while?"

"Yeah, that."

"Oh-kay," he said, still beaming.

"We should probably go back to the house. I don't want to leave Baxi alone too long."

"She might get into trouble."

"I think she's old enough that she doesn't need someone watching her all the time, but I won't wear her down if I'm not around her."

"I like how you think, Amina," he said thoughtfully. "You're stubborn. I'll give you that."

Stubborn enough to make a twelve-year-old like me by the day after tomorrow?

Surprisingly, Baxi hung out in the kitchen while I made dinner with Krill, though she didn't volunteer to help, and she ignored me when I asked if she wanted to stir the sauce.

Still, she sat at the table with me, Krill, and Thul, eating everything on her plate, and she didn't even snarl when I offered her a big slice of chocolate cake.

Maybe she was thawing. Or maybe I was reading

more into this than I should. I had tomorrow and part of the day after that to get her to a point where she'd tell the agent she was okay with me staying. I assumed that's what she'd say. I doubted they'd expect her to love me or anything like that. But if she stated she could tolerate me mating with her dad, they'd probably sign off on my case.

After dinner, Krill read while Thul and I watched a show about animals in the Sahara on TV. Baxi remained with us, staring at the screen, saying nothing, not even when her dad asked if she'd ever want to adopt a fennec fox.

"Me, me," Krill shouted, showing that even while reading, he was still paying attention to what was going on around him. "Let's leave tomorrow to get one."

"Can we wait until Saturday?" I asked. We hadn't told the children the agent was coming and that she'd ask them questions as well. We'd decided to wait until she was about to arrive and explain then. No need for them to stress about this.

Although, Baxi might salivate at the chance to tell the agent she hated me. Assuming she still did. She hadn't made eye contact all night, but she'd almost been pleasant.

I could live with that.

When it started to rain and thunder rang out, Thul and I skipped going to the pool. I wanted to be with him, and we had the rest of our lives. It was nice sitting with him in the evening, watching a show on TV like we were an old married couple. Plenty of time for hot and heavy in the future.

Besides, I suspected by tomorrow, he'd have plenty of peristyle tea . . .

Tomorrow night was going to be amazing, and the day after that? We'd breeze through the last test and sail into a full mating. I had to believe that, or I'd fret.

The kids went to bed, and we watched another show, this one called Generation Gap, a family comedy about the clashes between generations living under one roof. The grandparents tried to understand new technology, while the kids navigated school dramas. We laughed all the way through it and that lightened my mood.

"How are things going?" Thul asked after we'd shut off the TV.

I knew what he meant. "It wasn't bad today. She's not exactly friendly, but she's not snarling or acting like she hates me. Progress."

"Enough for the day after tomorrow?"

I shrugged. "I'm not sure what the agent will want to hear from the kids. I hope Baxi will tell her that she's okay with me remaining here. I'll settle for that."

He nodded and turned to face me, his tail looping around my waist. He lifted me and placed me on his lap, the best place to be in the world.

I snuggled into his arms, and when we started to kiss, I lost track of everything around me.

He lowered me onto the cushions and followed, where his gentle strokes heated me up fast.

"I miss our swim," he growled into my throat.

"Soon. Shall we have a tea party tomorrow?"

"I'll go into town first thing and get it. Drink it, and then, you can do with me as you please."

"I want it all, Thul."

"Even if something happens with the bureau?"

I clung to his shoulders. "They won't rip us apart. I won't let them."

"I've got a back-up plan if they try something like that."

"What is it?"

"I'll let you know if I need to activate it." He nuzzled my neck. "More kisses, please."

I happily gave in to his request.

But while we could make out on the sofa, we couldn't do anything to heavy, not when one of the kids might walk in on us at any minute. And taking it to his bedroom didn't feel right yet. Once our mating was approved, however, I was going to pack up my things and truck them over to his bedroom. After that, I was never leaving.

He kissed me again outside my bedroom and stroked my face. "See you in the morning?"

"I'll make something tasty."

"You're tasty, and that's all I need."

With a smile on my face, I went into my room and got ready in the adjoining bathroom. I shut out the light and climbed under the covers, stretching out.

Something tickled my arm. Something else teased across my thigh.

I bolted from the bed and snapped on the light, flinging back the covers.

Three big spiders the size of my fist scrambled across my sheets.

CHAPTER 24
THUL

The next morning, Baxi joined us in the kitchen much earlier than normal. Odd, since she was the one who most enjoyed sleeping in.

She sat at the island and watched Amina intently as my mate prepared breakfast, something called coffee cake, though it had no coffee grounds in it. Amina hummed and shifted her hips to a tune she hummed under her breath, pausing in the cooking process to take sips of her coffee.

The cake that wasn't a true cake but a breakfast bread was in the oven, she turned and leaned against the counter.

"What's your favorite subject in school, Baxi?" she asked pleasantly. "I used to love social studies."

Baxi frowned.

When she didn't answer, I nudged her thigh gently.

"Math," Baxi barked out.

This was the first time I'd heard she liked math. Last I knew, it was her least favorite subject.

"Science," she added. "And world government."

"So many great subjects to study." Amina smiled and brought her coffee over, placing it on the island.

Baxi reeled backward. "I didn't do it!"

"Do what?" I asked, looking between them. Something odd was going on here.

"Nothing." Baxi shot a look toward the wing with our bedrooms. "I didn't do anything and there's nothing to talk about."

All right. "Krill loves science," I said as my son joined us.

"No I don't." He crinkled his face Amina's way. "I like reading. And more reading. Any subject, and while I've been a sci-fi geek for ages, I believe I'm now partial to fantasy. Although, I don't like how some authors handle monsters. I mean, dragons do not regularly fry people and trolls are super-nice, not snarly."

"That's good to hear." Amina's eyes sparkled with humor. "I assume from that statement that trolls and dragons exist."

"Sure they do." Krill grunted. "And unicorns haven't died out. They're not magical, however. They're basically horses with rainbow manes and tails. They eat tons of grass and poop a lot."

Amina leaned forward to ruffle his hair. "You don't say?"

"I *do* say."

"What about brownies?" she asked.

"Yum."

"I was speaking of the small people who clean while you're asleep."

He shook his head. "Now *that's* just a fairy tale."

"Bummer. We could've left them some treats and maybe they'd vacuum, something I need to do today. Someone keeps tracking in mud on my newly clean floors."

Baxi's face darkened. "It wasn't me!"

"I'm not accusing you," Amina said. "Of anything."

"Why not?" Tears sprung up in Baxi's eyes.

"Because I don't do things like that."

"Well maybe you should." With that, Baxi sobbed. She slid off her stool and raced to her room, though she didn't slam her door.

"See?" Krill said. "A total pisser."

CHAPTER 25
AMINA

After Thul left for his lab, I cleaned up what was left of the coffee cake and did the dishes. But when I dragged the vacuum out of the closet, Baxi appeared by my side. She snatched the hose from me and plugged the vacuum in, then started to suck up the clumps of dirt near the door.

"Why did you do it?" I asked over the roar.

"Sorry." She shot me a neutral look before returning her gaze to her work. "Can't hear you over the motor." With considerable vigor, she continued running the wand all over the living room floor, the kitchen tiles, and the hallways.

I watched, but before she could start on the bedrooms, I went over and pulled the plug out of the wall. I gathered it, wrapping it around my arm in coils until I'd tugged Baxi and the vacuum back into the living room.

When she rolled her eyes, I did the same.

I pointed to the sofa. "Sit."

With a grumble, she did, and I joined her. She shifted sideways to ensure our bodies weren't touching, staring forward.

"Why did you do it?" I asked gently.

"Do what?" The shake of her hands gave her away.

"You know what I'm talking about."

"They weren't the poisonous kind."

"How delightful." I couldn't suppress my shiver. "You should've seen me trying to scoop them up with a piece of paper and take them outside."

Her head tilted, and she glanced my way. "Why not just kill them and throw them in the toilet?"

"Because they're alive."

"So was the gator that was made into sausage, but I don't see you delicately taking that outside to let it go free."

"That's a good point." I frowned. "Does this mean you no longer want to eat meat?"

She groaned. "I didn't say that."

"You could live on cookies."

"And chocolate cake," she said with a huff.

I chuckled. "Thanks for not putting poisonous spiders in my bed."

"You're welcome."

"I know you did it to try to drive me away, and I want to say that it made me feel sad, not mad."

"Sad?"

"Yeah. Silly me. When I came here, I had such high hopes. I like your dad a lot, and I planned to do all I could to show you and your brother that I wanted to be friends. I knew your mom had died, and I never wanted to do anything that might suggest I was trying to take her place."

Her lips twisted. "You're not doing *that* horrible a job."

"That's just it. It's not a job. I'm not your nanny. I'm someone who just wants a chance to make your father happy."

She said nothing for a long while. "I do want Dad to be happy."

"Even if that means I stay in your life?"

Her sigh bled out. "I wish Mom was here. We were a family. Now we're just pieces of what we were before and none of them fit together like they used to."

"I'm sorry. I wish I'd had the chance to meet her."

"Yeah."

"Do you think we can form a truce?" I held my breath, waiting for her to speak.

"I don't want to."

My shoulders sagged.

"But I guess I could try," she said.

Now would not be the time to leap around with joy. "I appreciate it." That was a nice, neutral thing to say.

"Don't think this means I like you or anything like that."

My chest would hurt if I didn't see the upward twitch of her lips. This child used subtle humor like a well-hewn blade.

"I'll keep that in mind," I said.

Finally, she faced me, though her gaze didn't meet mine. "Why didn't you tell Dad what I did?"

"Because this is between you and me."

"He would've punished me for doing it. I would've told him for sure."

I was an adult, not a child, and my goal here wasn't to get her into trouble but to get along with her. I liked her despite her snarls. I wanted to know her better, to be a part of raising her to be a young female Thul would be proud of—of one *I'd* be proud of too.

"Would complaining to your dad make you accept me?" I asked.

"Not in the least."

Then it was good that I didn't do it. "Next time, if you really want to hear me shriek, use snakes."

She shivered. "I'm not touching snakes."

I could be grateful for that.

Baxi rose. "I guess I should finish vacuuming."

Hope bloomed anew in my chest, and my throat was suddenly so tight, I couldn't suck in a deep breath. "Thanks for the help," I croaked.

She grunted as she walked over to the vacuum cleaner. "It's the least I can do since I tracked in the mud."

CHAPTER 26

THUL

Something changed between me leaving to work in my lab and returning at the end of the day in time for dinner.

Baxi was not hiding in her room.

She, Krill, and Amina were making dinner. Not only that, but they were also singing a song about a swamp thing making their hearts sing.

Krill pretended to play the drums with two wooden spoons thudding on the bottom of a salad bowl, and Baxi gyrated, holding a ladle as if it was a microphone.

I heeled off my shoes and glanced back at the front door. "Have I come to the wrong house?"

"Dad," Krill sighed. "That's a very poor joke."

I strode forward in bare feet. "I think it's cute." Sidling up to Amina, I nuzzled her neck.

Baxi and Krill watched us raptly. It was a test—of sorts. I wanted to do this with Amina all the time, and I didn't want to hide the fact that I craved her. But I didn't want to gross my children out—*gross out* being a Krill term. I sensed something had changed here, and I wanted to test my new theory. "What do you think, sweet one?" I slid her hair to the side and kissed the nape of her neck. "Am I cute?"

"Incredibly," she croaked, turning to face me. She fanned her face, and I wanted to kiss the color rising in her cheeks. But I wasn't quite ready to take my theory that far.

Baxi sighed but unbelievably enough, pushed for a smile. She did turn away, however, and I was glad I hadn't taken this very far.

"Yuck," Krill said. "Back to making yum." He stirred whatever was cooking on the stove.

"Smells amazing." I gave Amina a grin she returned. My heart tripped over itself, and I decided nothing could be better than this moment with my family.

"We're having tuber soup," Baxi said. "Mom's recipe." She shot Amina a look I couldn't define, though she looked almost happy. "Amina suggested we make it tonight."

"The frog's legs were my downfall," Amina sighed.

"In what way?" Turning, I leaned against the counter beside her.

"Krill caught them."

"And squished them," he said fiercely, making a fist. "Not too much. I'm not cruel."

"Baxi kindly took care of cleaning them," Amina said.

"And without being too squeamish, Amina cut them

up and sauteed them in butter," Baxi said. "We . . ." Her eyes closed for a moment, and when she opened them, they sparkled with tears, but she gave me a true smile. "You always loved it when Mom made this stew."

Something had happened, but I wasn't going to jinx it by naming it. "I can't wait to taste it."

"It might not be as good as what your mom used to make," Amina said, adding dried swamp greens to the steaming broth. "But I wanted to make something everyone would enjoy." She nudged her head to a square pan with yellow cake. "I made cornbread to go with it."

"I've never had cornbread," I said, wondering where the corn cobs went. Hopefully, they weren't ground up and added as chunks to the mix. If they were, I'd smile while I ate it, because pleasing Amina was a big goal in my life.

"It smells good, and that's all I need," Krill said. He gave me a sunny smile. "I love trying new human recipes."

"And I'm enjoying swamp monster food." Amina got out bowls and after shutting off the burner, ladled out servings for each of us, even a full bowl for herself.

We sat at the table and ate, groaning about how good everything was. I, on the side, was grateful not to find chunks of corn cob in the bread that really was more like cake with a subtle crunch. Were any human foods true to their names?

After cleaning everything up, we worked on a puzzle at the island, even Baxi.

I began to think everything was going to be all right.

Just in time, because Agent Barclest would be here to administer the final test tomorrow.

CHAPTER 27

AMINA

The kids went to bed, and Thul and I sat close together on the sofa.

"Guess what I got in town today?" he asked softly.

I shrugged.

"The healer has returned."

My heart tripped over itself. "And . . ."

"I drank my first cup of peristyle tea this afternoon."

"How long before its effective?"

He gave me such a sultry smile; it made my pulse surge through the roof. "Your eggs are safe from my lecturs right now."

Oh, fuck.

I mean, *fuck*.

"We can do it," I breathed.

"Only if you're ready. No pressure. We're still getting to know each other."

I cocked my head. "Do you feel like you need to know me better to make a decision about something like this?"

"I love you, Amina. I don't need more time. But I also would never do something if you weren't one hundred percent into it."

I grinned. "Why are we wasting time sitting here on the sofa?"

He stood, swept me up into his arms, and raced toward the front door. It clicked shut behind him, and he didn't stop, but ran around our home, along the path and past his lab, heading down the trail leading to the pool.

"I take it you're not wasting any time," I quipped.

"Not any longer." He came to a stop beside the pool, not even breathing fast after running. "You're completely sure?"

"I need you, Thul. I love you. Show me the world."

He gently placed me on my feet and removed my clothing, flinging his own aside.

I gazed down at his cock thrusting against his abs, and despite its size, I couldn't wait to feel it, to join with him completely.

Taking him in my hand, I ran my fingertips up and down his length, gliding my thumb across the precum coating the tip.

"Amina," he growled. His tail lifted me, and we kissed, his tongue sliding into my mouth to heat me up even further. His fingers traced across my breasts, and he cupped them, pinching the nipples just enough to make them form hard buds.

I moaned and arched my back, urging his face down to my breasts.

He sucked on one nipple, then the other, tugging gently with his fangs.

There couldn't be anything better than this, but his cock . . .

With me in his arms, he strode into the water until we floated, turning me so I could hold on to his shoulders.

His tail teased between my legs while his mouth captured mine once more. It glided across my clit, making me gasp. When his fingers slid inside my passage, I groaned again. I shifted my hips against him, unable to believe we'd finally reached this moment. It was pure yet gritty, and I wouldn't have it any other way.

He moved us over to a ledge projecting into the water and placed me on it, springing up onto the smooth surface beside me. Spreading my legs, he shot me a smile before he moved around until he was between my thighs. When he stroked my clit with his tongue, I jerked out a moan.

"You taste amazing. I need more," he growled. His tongue slid inside me, flickering against my inner walls.

I bucked up against him, and when I started to fall apart, he moved his tongue faster, taking me to the moon and back in one fell swoop.

CHAPTER 28
THUL

When her inner walls stopped spasming, I rose above her and spread her legs, crawling between them.

My cock was on fire. I pressed it against the entrance to her passage, groaning at how tight and wet she was. It was all I could do not to plunge inside, to ride her welcoming body until we both exploded.

"Take me," she said, her gaze locking on mine. "I need to feel you. Know you. I want everything."

When she locked her heels around my waist, I slid the tip of my tail over to her clit. It was hard and tight from her orgasm, and I rubbed it while she shifted her hips up.

I pushed forward, gliding the head of my cock deeper into her hot sheath.

She gasped. "More."

My eyeballs rolled back in my head. I'd never felt anything as amazing as this. But I needed more. Pulling back, I drove my cock forward, seating it fully inside her. My lecturs coiled and twisted inside my length, and it was all I could do not to release them.

They teased out of the head, gliding against her inner walls as I moved in and out of her.

She cried out, and I echoed it with a groan. A fever rose inside me, and nothing was going to keep me from claiming her fully. Her head thrashing on the ledge, she urged me on with tight grips on my forearms and her hips jutting up to meet each of my thrusts.

Need churned through my blood, and a bead of sweat coiled down my brow.

My tail continued to stroke her clit as I moved within her.

She was everything I could ever need, so precious and responsive.

I moved faster, driving myself into her welcome heat over and over.

When she shuddered around my cock like a fist tightening its grip, I gave way, releasing my lecturs. They spiraled upward, seeking her womb, and while they'd still plant pods deep within her, the pods had been neutralized.

She wouldn't get pregnant, not until we both agreed it was time for me to stop drinking the tea.

I collapsed on her, my cock pulsing as the lecturs moved higher.

"I wasn't sure how this part would feel," she said breathlessly. "But . . ." Her moan ripped out as she orgasmed once more. "I have a feeling I'm going to love your lecturs as much as I do you."

My laugh spurted out. "You're perfect, mate. Utterly perfect."

I rolled until she lay across my chest, my cock still locked within her. The lecturs would coil back inside me soon, and my body would release hers.

Until then, I savored how complete I felt for the first time in my life.

CHAPTER 29

AMINA

Thul and I made love a bunch more times, staying at the pool for hours. Were we fulfilling the heat he'd spoken of? If so, it had consumed me as much as him. I couldn't get enough.

"We should probably head back soon," he said, teasing the tip of his tail across my belly.

My laugh quavered out, and I nudged his tail away. If I happened to push it lower, so be it.

He rolled onto his back, taking me with him, and I spread my legs around his hips.

"Or perhaps we should delay returning home," he rasped, lifting his head to give me a kiss.

I was soon fully absorbed by the movement of his mouth and the way his tongue coiled around mine. His tail glided across my clit, and when it started to dip inside me, I nudged it away and wrapped my hand around his erect cock.

Rising, I placed it at my opening, and with our gazes

locked together, I sunk down onto him, taking every-thing he had to offer. Our groans rang out.

I started to lift and fall back, and his hands on my hips added pressure to my fall. He was embedded deep within me, and already, I could feel his lecturs twisting around at the tip. Each time I rose, they glided across my G-spot, and my eyes soon rolled back in my head.

I rode him as fast as I could while he jerked his hips up to meet me.

And when we fell apart together, I collapsed on his chest, kissing his neck.

"Mate," he growled. "I'm going to crave your touch for the rest of my days."

"Good, because I know I can't live without yours."

WE DRESSED, and he insisted on carrying me back to our home, where we crept inside. Stopping outside my room, he pressed me against the wall and stroked my face.

"Soon, our mating will be approved," he said against my neck.

"And then I can move into your room." No more sleeping apart. No more sneaking around to be together. "I can't wait."

He kissed me fast. "You tempt me very much."

I fanned my face, overheated already. At this rate, I'd need a cold shower—or another run with him to the pool.

"Until tomorrow," he said, his words a promise I took to my heart.

After stroking his chest, I went inside. I slept better than I had since I'd arrived. Since I was nervous about the agent's visit, I woke early, laying in my bed while dawn split the world wide open and streaked yellow, red, and gold across the sky. I wasn't as scared about this as I'd been the day before. Baxi and I had made progress. But was it enough?

She might still tell the agent she hated me, that she wanted me to leave.

Grumbling about it, I slipped from bed, showered and dressed, and headed to the kitchen. Maybe a nice breakfast would set the stage for a good day, not one where I'd end up packing my bags and moving out.

It didn't take long to mix up batter for waffles. We'd bought the waffle iron while in town, but I hadn't used it yet. Soon, it was heating, and I had oil ready to brush on both sides to keep my waffles from sticking. Syrup was warming in a pan on the stove, and I'd gotten the butter out of the fridge to give it time to soften.

Krill appeared first; his nose lifted to sniff the air. "Do I smell yum?"

I rounded the island and gave him a big hug, lifting him off his feet. "You smell lots of yum."

"Why the spontaneous gesture?" he asked, blushing as I placed him back on his feet. "Not that I'm complaining, though don't do it around my friends too often."

"I promise never to embarrass you." I made an X on my chest for good measure. "Cross my heart."

"What can I do to help?" Thul asked as he strode out of the hallway looking like a mossy green lollipop in need of a good licking. Man, did he look amazing in snug jeans and green t-shirt. Almost as good as when he wore nothing.

"You could get out plates and silverware, plus napkins. Krill, would you see if your sister's up and hungry? Nicely." I called out as he raced down the hall toward her room. "Don't rile her up!"

"It doesn't take much," Thul said. "Though I sensed a change in the air that'll be good for all of us."

I could only hope it lasted.

I lifted the latest waffle from the iron, placed it on the platter to the right, brushed on more oil and added batter, smiling as it sizzled. With the iron closed, it started to cook.

Turning, I leaned against the counter. "What time do you think she'll be here today?"

"I assume first thing, so nine-ish."

A glance at the clock told me we had an hour. Bees kept buzzing around in my belly, and I could only hope they didn't sting.

Krill returned and sat on a stool. "She's coming. She's not a pisser this morning either. If she had been, I would've told her to knock it off."

Baxi appeared wearing PJs. "What's all the fuss about this morning? I was sleeping in."

"Lots of yum is enough reason for anyone to get up," Krill said, wiggling on his stool. "How much longer until we can gorge ourselves?"

I moved the last waffle to the platter and shut the iron off. With the enormous stack teetering on the plate, I strode over to the table, presenting the meal with a flourish. "Voila!'

"They look great." Baxi sent me a shy smile and the bees who'd taken up residence in my belly settled to watch and wait.

With a happy sigh, I joined them, placing a waffle on my plate, slathering it with butter and syrup, and stuffing a big bite into my mouth.

"Wonderful," Baxi mumbled around a bit. "Almost as good as coffeecake."

"Better," Krill said, eyeing the rest of the pile. "Two each. We're gonna have to make more!"

We chowed through the pile, which seemed to be enough for this morning, and I promised to make waffles again soon.

After we'd cleaned up, Thul cleared his throat. "I have an announcement to make."

Baxi had started toward the kitchen to take care of her plate, but she paused, looking back. Her frown went from him to me, but she said nothing.

"Agent Barclest is coming here today to give Amina her final test," he said.

Krill relaxed in a chair, opening a book on his lap. "She's going to do great."

"This test has one extra component." I sucked in a breath and spit the rest out with the air. "She'll ask you two for your thoughts about me."

"Like, if I tell her I hate you, she'll make you leave?" Baxi asked.

The bees in my belly started buzzing again.

"Yes," I said in a small voice.

Krill glared her way. "If you say that, I'm going to hate you forever. I like Amina. I want her to stay."

Thul came over and wrapped his arm around my shoulders. "So do I."

"If she'd asked me when you arrived," Baxi said. "I would've told her that." She shrugged. "I wouldn't say that now, Krill."

"Good." He buried his nose in his book.

"Anyway," I said. "We just wanted you to know so you'd be prepared."

A car pulled into the driveway, tires crunching on the gravel. It was followed by a door slamming shut.

"She's here." Thul turned to face me, cupping my cheeks. "You have nothing to worry about."

He was right. It looked like this was going to be a breeze.

CHAPTER 30

THUL

Before we let the agent inside, we'd sent Krill and Baxi to their rooms but asked them to be ready once the second interview was over.

Krill nodded. "Nothing to it; it's done and Amina's staying."

Baxi's gaze traveled between me and Amina and while she didn't say anything before entering her room, she didn't glare. I took that as a good sign.

We let Agent Barclest in and settled on the sofa with her taking the chair opposite us. She beamed before pulling her questionnaire and pen from her bag with her tail.

"What do you find the most appealing about swamp monster culture, and how would you embrace it as part of your everyday life?" she asked.

Amina cleared her throat and squeezed my hand. Hers trembled, and I put my arm around her shoulders for support. "The more I've gotten to know swamp monster culture, the more captivated I've been by the connection to nature. This aligns with my own values, and I plan to immerse myself in learning traditional swamp monster ecological practices such as specific plants crucial to the ecosystem, as well as sustainability. I believe this will deepen the bond with my new family."

The agent nodded thoughtfully, and from the pleased look she sent me, I could tell Amina was doing well already.

"The next question." She frowned at her clipboard and read. "This one relates to Thul's children. Are there any specific challenges or difficulties that might arise while interacting with them and how would you handle those situations?"

"I think there will be lots of challenges. They're children and each is unique and needs a different sort of support. I can honestly say that I care deeply for both of them already, and I hope to continue taking a role in raising them to be happy adults. But as to your question," she paused and glanced down at her lap before looking up again, "I've already had some challenges with Baxi, Thul's daughter. Initially, she thought I was here to step into her late mother's shoes, so to speak. While she's resisted my being here, we've managed to establish understanding and respect. A truce, you could say."

"How did you do this?"

"I acknowledged her emotions and gave her space. Isn't that what all children need? I made sure she knows I want to honor her mother's memory, not take her place."

Baxi's door opened, and she came down the hall. "Can I get some water?"

"Sure," I said. "I believe we're almost through."

"We are." The agent nodded toward Baxi. "Will you have a few moments soon to chat?"

Baxi's gaze met mine, and the calm I read there reassured me. She filled a glass at the sink.

"And the final question, though it's a mere formality now." The agent beamed, and I relaxed fully. "Do you have any concerns about balancing individual identities after you've mated with Thul? I speak of those related to personal aspirations or goals."

Baxi went to the cupboard and started sorting through things. Hungry already? But she was a growing swamp monster, and her mother had been almost as tall as me.

Amina shot a smile my way, and reading the open affection there made my heart thump faster. I tightened my arm around her shoulders. I'd be grateful when this was over, and we could start our new life together without worrying something might tear us apart.

"I think the best way for me and Thul to strike a balance together is through good communication. I'm excited to support his scientific endeavors in any way I can, and I'm confident he's equally happy to encourage me while I achieve my own goals."

"Definitely," I chimed in.

Baxi grunted but didn't look our way.

"Our shared passion for knowledge is going to play a big part in helping us understand each other's aspirations better," Amina said. She rubbed my thigh, and I suppressed my stupid cock that so easily responded to her touch. "By talking about our ambitions and dreams, we can work together to find ways toward achieving them together while leaving room for the growth we both need. I think that's the key to both of us flourishing."

"Excellent," Agent Barclest said, laying her clipboard on the coffee table. "We're finished, and you've done well, Amina. All that's left is the quick interview with your children, Thul. If you'll—"

"How could you, Dad?" Baxi barked. She strode over to stand in front of us, dangling the big bag of peristyle tea. "How could you think about having sex with Amina?" Her glare slid between us. "I hate you both!"

She flung the tea onto the floor and raced to her room.

CHAPTER 31
AMINA

"I'll go talk with her," Thul said.

My heart had sunk to the bottom of the swamp. I had a feeling this interview was over, and I'd failed.

My eyes kept brimming with tears. I loved Thul. I wanted to be with him. But if his children didn't approve, it was impossible. I never wanted to come between them.

"Can I speak with her instead?" I asked.

Agent Barclest stared at us with wide eyes, saying nothing.

Thul studied my face. "Are you sure?"

"Maybe it would be best. If I can't reason with her now, how am I going to do it when she's a teenager or an adult?"

"I can wait," the agent said in a chilling voice.

Damn, I'd blown it. We were so close.

I sniffed back my tears and rose, walking down the hall to Baxi's room, where I knocked on her door.

"Go away," she called out.

I opened the door and stepped inside, closing it behind me.

"Why don't you ever listen?" she said.

"Because I think it's time you listened to me." I walked over and sat in the chair near her bed. She lay on the surface, turned toward the wall.

"I hate you. I hate Dad too. You're so gross. How could you have sex with him?"

"Because I love him."

She sucked in a breath. "It's still gross."

"I imagine to a twelve-year-old, it is. Not to me."

"I don't care about your feelings."

"I'm sorry to hear that." My voice cratered with grief. "Because I care about *your* feelings. I want to get to know you, Baxi, to be here when you leap into your teen years, for when you go on your first date. I want to be here with you when you pick out colleges, if that's what you choose to do. I want to be with you if you decide to mate. And I want to hold any tads you might deliver, if something wonderful like that should happen. But if you truly hate me because I love your dad, I have to wonder what I can do or say that might actually make a difference."

She remained silent. Was she even listening?

"If you want me to leave, I will," I said. "From the start, I told myself I'd never force this, that your acceptance was just as important as your dad's or your brother's."

"You'll walk out that easily? So much for being in love with my dad."

"It's because I love him that I'll walk out, as you put it. What do you think it will do to him to see us squabbling all the time, for him to think you hate me?"

She didn't answer. Hopefully that was because she was hearing and thinking.

"I don't want him to be forced to choose between us, and I never want to put you in a situation where you have to pick either." I rose. "Go ahead and tell the agent whatever you want. Speak from your heart because that's what she wants to hear. I respect you, and that means I'm going to do my best to respect your decision."

With that, I walked from her room. I kept going, not saying anything when Thul called out as I passed. Outside my home, I walked stiffly around the mound. It was only when I reached the path toward the pond that I broke into a run. I kept going until I reached the shore.

I dropped to the ground and stared at the water. My chest ached, and I rubbed it. Tears fell down my face, and I ignored them.

I'd said what I needed to. The decision was no longer mine to make.

How could our love survive this challenge?

CHAPTER 32
THUL

I went and knocked on Krill's door. He came out with a smile and skipped into the living room to speak with Agent Barclest. I didn't follow. Instead, I went into Baxi's room and sat on the edge of her bed.

I didn't ask questions, and I didn't speak. Finally, she turned to face me. Seeing tears on her face pretty broke me.

When I held out my arms to her, she tumbled into them and sobbed.

While Baxi spoke with the agent, I found Amina sitting beside the pool and dropped down beside her. I tugged her into my arms and held her, savoring the peace I'd only found in this location and the love I felt for this woman.

"I'm sorry," she whispered. "Maybe we should've waited before being together fully."

"The conversation was going to happen. I love you. You love me. It's natural for us to be together in all ways." I sighed. "I'd hoped she'd come around, that she'd see how amazing you are, how perfect you are for me."

She turned in my arms and wrapped her legs around me. Tears had dried on her cheeks, and I hated seeing them there. Both of the females I loved were hurting, and it didn't seem like there was anything I could do to make this better.

"I'll pack my things," Amina said.

"I don't want you to go."

"If it was about just us, we wouldn't need to have this conversation, but your children's feelings are equally important."

"I love you, Amina." It was all I could say. Vowing to snarl at my daughter, to make her accept Amina, would do none of us any good.

"It hurts," she said. "I love you, and I want to make a life with you."

"We deserve this chance."

"Very much. But what do your children deserve? We have to think of them too."

And there it was. My heart felt splayed wide open, sliced to pieces and exposed to the harshest elements, and there was nothing I could do to repair it.

I rose with her in my arms and carried her back to the house. The agent must be done speaking with Baxi by now.

Lowering her to her feet outside the door, I nudged it open, and we stepped inside.

"Ah, there you are." Agent Barclest stood in the living room, peering around.

Krill, as usual, sat in a chair, reading a book.

Baxi sat on the sofa, staring at the floor beneath the coffee table.

"I'll be on my way, then," the agent said. She bustled over and stopped beside us, her tail sweeping back and forth. "The paperwork will be processed soon, and you two can make your plans."

To move Amina out? I gazed at her starkly, taking in her pretty form, her lush curves I'd love completely, and the sadness in her eyes. I held her hand, and I didn't want to let it go, fearing if I did, she'd slip away, and I'd never see her again.

"Do either of you have any questions?" the agent asked. When we remained silent, she left. The roar of her car echoed around us, followed by the crunch of tires in the drive. Soon, the sound of her engine faded.

"I told her I love you, Amina," Krill said, closing his book. "That you make excellent waffles, but even more than that, that I know that you love me just as much as I do you."

"Aw, Krill." Amina sniffed and went over to stoop down beside his chair, ruffling his hair. "Thanks."

I looked at Baxi, striving to keep my expression neutral. She was an equal member of this family, and her opinion mattered. I couldn't let my disappointment shine on my face, though it rumbled around in my chest.

"I told her I wanted Amina to stay," Baxi said softly.

Amina's breath caught, and she rose to her feet, reaching out to grab onto the back of Krill's chair as if she was worried she'd fall. "You did?"

"You did?" I pretty much bellowed.

"I'm not mean. I listen. I think." Baxi's chin lifted, and she got to her feet. Would she run into her room and slam her door, shutting us out again? "I also make my own decisions. And unlike what Krill thinks, I'm *not* a pisser."

"I'll concede you're only a pisser sometimes," he said with a grin that took us all in. Jumping to his feet, he raced around the room three times. "There. Had to get that out of my system. The tension was alive in the room!"

I gaped at Baxi and held out my arms to Amina. When she stepped inside them, I held her. I wasn't going to let go for a very long time.

"It's over, right?" Krill asked, stopping beside us. "Amina's tests are finished, no one messed up, even my sister, and now she can stay forever."

"Yup, it's over," I croaked. "It's . . . wonderful, actually. Everything. You, your sister, and Amina."

"You too, Dad." Krill beamed up at Amina.

How had I lucked into having her and my children in my life?

I leaned over and captured Amina's mouth with my own, savoring how amazing she tasted, how she pressed herself against me. When I finally came up for air, Krill clapped.

"I like seeing you two happy, but could you hold off on all that gross stuff for a moment?" he said with a twist of his face.

"I'll try," I said gravely.

"You." Amina smiled his way.

"So now we're a real family?" he asked, though his gaze sought out his sister.

She jerked her head in a nod.

"Okay, then, big hug time!" He barreled into me and Amina and reached out to Baxi.

She sighed and got up to join us, and while her lips remained pinched, her eyes shone with the beginning of joy.

"Come on, sis," Krill said. "Put some effort into it."

Baxi's arm tightened around me, and from the look on Amina's face, she felt it too.

"If you're nice to Amina," Krill added, "I bet she'll make you some cookies."

"Many batches," Amina said. She curled her finger my way, and when I lowered my head, she gave me a kiss. It was sweet, pure, and it sparked heat deep inside me.

And that's when I knew things were going to be all right.

As Krill said, we were now a family.

CHAPTER 33
EPILOGUE
AMINA

Two Years Later

"There, take a look," I said, stepping away from Baxi, the duloppir brush lifted in my hand. "I think I did okay."

Baxi turned and peered into the bathroom mirror, taking in the patterns I'd carefully painted onto her shoulders and neck. The duloppir herb would remain there until it dried, after which, she'd wash off the excess and the lines would remain for weeks. "It looks amazing."

She whirled around and gave me a hug.

I held her, savoring how wonderful it was to do things like this with my stepdaughter.

In the two years since me and Thul celebrated our full mating, Baxi and Krill had grown taller and all of us had grown closer. Tonight, Baxi was going on her first date, though at fourteen, it wasn't a true date. The school was holding a dance, and a young yeti male had asked her if she'd be there. When she said yes, he'd tipped his head back, bellowed, then sweetly kissed her thumb tip —a yeti tradition that meant he liked her.

Since she liked him too, she'd wanted to dress up to look her best. Patterns on her skin was a swamp monster tradition for young ladies.

Thul waited in the living room. Or paced in the living room. He'd give her a ride to the dance and pick her up after, and he was a wreck. His little girl was growing up, and he wasn't sure he liked it.

"Are you sure you're feeling okay?" she asked, her happy gaze going to my big belly. I'd deliver our first tad soon, and we all couldn't wait, even Baxi, who insisted she was going to be the best big sister possible. Krill wasn't so sure about that . . . Although, he'd stopped calling Baxi a pisser not long after me and Thul cele-brated our mating. A win all around.

"I feel amazing," I said.

"Don't overdo it."

"I agree." Thul stood the open doorway. "You're precious, and you should sit with your feet up while we run around you, fetching whatever you need."

If he had his way, I wouldn't do a thing. But I loved taking care of my family.

"Wow, Baxi." He tugged her near, spun her around, and admired the etchings I'd made on her skin. "No swamp monster mom could do better."

"Right." Baxi preened in the mirror. "Thanks so much, Amina." She gave me another hug and skipped out of the room. While it dried, she'd make sure everything else was ready in her bedroom to get ready.

"I think I'll go get a glass of water," I said.

Thul swept me off my feet. "No need to overdo it." He carefully carried me out to the living room and placed me on the sofa, lifting each of my feet to put them on the coffee table. He held up his finger. "Wait there. I'll get your water. Or do you prefer tuber juice? What should it be?"

"Just water. Thanks."

"Anything else while I'm there?" He hurried into the kitchen.

Krill looked up from his book. "Do you think this is a bit excessive, Dad?" At ten, he was taller than his dad, and the healers said he still had some growing left to do. I adored him and was incredibly proud to call him my stepson.

"My legs work very well," I added, nodding to Krill, who grinned.

"I can't do enough for Amina," Thul said.

With a shake of his head, Krill rose and headed to his bedroom. "If I know you two, you'll soon be kissing, though why you need to bother now that she's carrying a tad is beyond me."

Yeah, one day, he'd find out.

While he still cringed to see us kiss, his eyes always shone with happiness.

"You'll be kissing someone before you know it," Thul

called out to him as he placed my water on the coffee table along with a plate of sliced fruit and breaded, deep fried julons—something I'd craved from the moment we tossed out the peristyle tea and let his lecturs do their thing.

"Yuck," Krill said, shutting his door.

Thul settled beside me on the sofa, tugging me up onto his lap. "What do you think, mate. Should we kiss?"

"We could do even more," I whispered, not wanting the kids to hear.

"I've got a plan," he said, standing with me in his arms. He carried me out of the house and all the way to the pool, where he delicately removed my clothing. Dropping to his knees, he placed his warm palms on my belly and kissed it. "How are you doing in there, tad?"

The ultrasound showed we had just one, which was fine with us. I couldn't imagine having six or seven at one time like some swamp monster females did.

"Perhaps I should lie down," I said, my knees weak from the feelings of love pouring through me for this male.

"I believe you should." He scooped me up and laid me gently on the shore.

Then he nudged my thighs apart and was soon licking. As my sighs of pleasure echoed around us, I marveled at how amazing life could be.

My swamp monster definitely made my heart sing.

He was my everything.

And nothing could be better than that.

I hope you've enjoyed Swamp Thing!
I'd never contemplated writing a swamp monster before,
but Thull & Amina's story was SO much fun!

What's next?
How about an orc 007?
You know you want to read Undercover Orc,
and now you can!
Scroll forward to read chapter one.

Be sure to check out the rest of the books
in Monster Mate Mayhem:

Hot Wolf in the City, Honey Phillips
Fretty Yeti, Ivy Tempest
Gargoyle Gripe, Sabrina Cassidy
Mounting The Minotaur, Jade Waltz
Swamp Thing, Ava Ross
Djinn And Bear It, Darci R. Acula
The Naga's Reluctant Bride, Jessica Grayson
Trolling For Love, Nessie Sreil

Sign up for my newsletter and I'll
send you Orc's Mate for FREE!

Feeling orc-ish?
Get Orc Charming for FREE as well!

And I've got another
FREE BOOK just for YOU!
Pick up
Escorting the Alien

About the Author

Ava Ross is a two-time *USA Today* Bestselling author who has written numerous titles, all of them featuring sweet and steamy romance. She fell for men with unusual features when she first watched Star Wars, where alien creatures have gone mainstream. She lives in New England with her husband (who is sadly not an alien, though he is still cute in his own way), her kids, and a few assorted pets.

ALSO BY AVA ROSS

Mail-Order Brides of Crakair

Brides of Driegon

Fated Mates of the Ferlaern Warriors

Fated Mates of the Xilan Warriors

Holiday with a Cu'zod Warrior

Galaxy Games

Alien Warrior Abandoned

Beastly Alien Boss

Bride of the Fae

A Sci-Fi Holiday Tail

Monsterville, USA

Monster on Board

(co-written with Alana Khan)

Love at First Orc

Monster Mate Hunt

Sweet Monster Treats

Brides of the Zuldrux Warriors

Monsters, PI

Shared Worlds:

A Monster Worth Fighting For

Mated to the Dragon

Craving Stardust

Dad Bod Dragon

Swamp Thing (You Make My Heart Sing)

Jasmine's Enchanted Genie

You can find her books on Amazon.

UNDERCOVER ORC

**She does't do anything spontaneous or wild
. . . until a hot orc dares her to try something new.**

Bailey: As head librarian in my small town, I take my job seriously. So when I hear a sound in the library's attic while I'm working late and alone, and then a big, green, muscular orc creeps up behind me, I smack him in the head with a stapler. After the theft of an ancient orc book on loan to the library, is it any wonder I'm skittish?

Katar explains he heard me scream and only wanted to help. He's . . . upset, and I guess I can't blame him.

He offers to help me discover who stole the book and we track down one clue after another. But when he dares me to give into my wild side, I start falling in love.

Katar: Being hit in the head with a stapler is an interesting way to meet my fated mate. That's who this prim and proper, incredibly gorgeous librarian is. I only came to town to discover who stole the ancient orc manuscript. Then I'll return to the orc kingdom forever. But the thought of leaving this curvy, delectable woman makes me want to snarl.

So I'm going to crack this case. I'm going to show Bailey how to let loose. And then I'm claiming her as my bride.

Undercover Orc is part of the both Ava's Monster, PI and the Sweet Monster Treats shared world. It's a sweet and steamy standalone romance featuring a cinnamon roll orc which a creative . . . (cough), stunning size difference, a prim librarian who sometimes *does* let loose, and plenty of humor and heat.

Be sure to explore the other titles in the collection:
Protected by the Orc, by Honey Phillips
Arrested by the Orc, by Michele Mills

CHAPTER ONE
BAILEY

A bang rang out in the library's attic overhead, and my heart froze.

Someone was inside the library with me.

A short time ago, I'd released a sigh of relief, and even the pile of work waiting for me on my desk couldn't steal my joy. I'd always savored the quiet and solitude I found in this quaint brick building, when I could sit, open a book, and dive into a magical world. Or stroll through the stacks, brushing my fingertips across the book spines.

Belle's beast had nothing on this place.

Rolling ladders? We had three.

Endless collections on every topic? We had you covered.

Cozy nooks for reading? We had five on this level.

Another subtle sound echoed from above.

Swallowing hard, I rose to my stockinged feet, and

crept to my door and swung it open, wincing when it creaked.

"Hello?" I croaked, my voice echoing back at me in the long hallway outside my office.

After the theft of the glorious tome on loan from the orc kingdom, I was skittish.

And angry. How dare someone break into the library and steal a book?

I waited to the count of ten and when I didn't hear anything further from upstairs, I returned to my desk.

An hour ago, after shooing every one out, I'd closed and locked all the doors and sunk into my big leather desk chair bequeathed to me by the prior head librarian, my beloved mentor and substitute mother, Helga Merry-weather. She died a year ago, and I missed her.

Imagine, me only twenty-eight years old and the new head librarian. If Helga hadn't put in a good word for me before she passed . . . . Well, I didn't want to think about that. The loss of her mattered much more than a job.

Steam swirled off the cup of Earl Grey tea I'd brewed and placed on my desk. As the sun slid away, leaving darkness peppered with a few stars behind, I sipped my tea while pouring through papers. Only the floor lamp behind me cut through the shadows—and just barely at that.

Maybe I'd imagined the sound.

Peering overhead, I waited, my stockinged feet curling in my shoes.

When it was clear I must've imagined the sound, I made a note to have the janitor set some mouse traps in the attic. I returned to the pile of papers, trying to make sense of why a shoe company had sent the library an invoice.

Low footsteps rang out and I gaped at the coffered ceiling, cringing. My mouth went dry, and fear tightened its grip on my spine.

If this was daytime and patrons were around, I'd use my most stern librarian voice to call out. No, I'd stomp up the back staircase, wrench open the door to the attic, and snarl at whoever thought they had the right to explore the upper level of the building. During daylight hours, it would be mischievous kids. Or a woman lost while trying to find the bathroom.

But after the building was locked up tight? I didn't want to imagine who it could be—not after the theft.

I pawed through my desk drawers, but I didn't carry a gun. Or a bow and arrows. Where was a switchblade when a girl needed one?

Shuffles upstairs were followed by a low thud.

Should I call 9-1-1? Of course. What was I thinking? I lifted my phone only to find I hadn't plugged it in during lunch like I'd planned and the battery was dead.

"Leave the building," I hissed, rising from my chair with my purse and phone in hand. The chair squeaked, but not loudly. Spying the black metal stapler that had also belonged to my predecessor, I latched onto it, clutching it to my chest like it was a shotgun ready to fire. I tiptoed to the door and carefully turned the knob.

The door needed to be lubed, and it creaked again as I tugged it open. Holding my breath, I pinched my eyes shut and remained motionless as if doing so would keep me from being seen.

Rapid footsteps echoed overhead.

My heart came to a shuddering halt before kicking into high gear. I bolted down the hallway toward the front of the building, wishing the back door didn't alarm when it was opened and that I could escape that way since it was closer.

Reaching the foyer, I skidded across the antique wooden floorboards that clicked and groaned beneath me. Damn old place I'd loved since I was six and I snuck into the library after school because I dreaded going home. Helga Merryweather caught me hiding on a window seat and handed me a book, the first Narnia. I read it, then the next, and soon I'd devoured them all. I came to the library almost every day after that and poured through the shelves for something new. It was only natural I get my master's degree in Library Science.

Gasping and with shrieks erupting from my throat, I reached the big glass front door. I scrambled with the three locks—cursing the orc security guard who'd insisted they be installed to protect their precious book. We all knew how that turned out.

Finally, I unlocked the door. I wrenched it open and stumbled out onto the big open stone deck beyond. I nearly fell on my kitten heels while rushing down the granite stairs, and I kicked them aside to run more easily when I reached the paved walkway.

Still clutching the stapler and my purse, I scrambled out into the parking lot.

Stomps rang out nearby, followed by a few grunts, but I didn't look. I wouldn't do so until I was sitting inside my car with the doors locked. Streetlights blazed beyond the lot, but they didn't shed enough light to do more than keep me from tripping over something. Certainly not enough to make me feel safe.

As I approached my vehicle, the only one in the lot, I grabbed my key fob, grateful I'd clipped it to my purse handle and hadn't buried it inside.

Wrong time to be thinking about being buried, Bailey, I thought as I drew closer to my car. The headlights flashed as I unlocked it, and with my purse swinging from my arm, I reached out for the door handle.

A hand dropped onto my shoulder.

Shrieking, I whirled, kicked the person in the shins, and chucked the stapler at the enormous, shadowy being.

It smacked against a tall orc's forehead.

Groaning, he dropped to his knees and tumbled onto his butt.

Get Undercover Orc NOW!

www.ingramcontent.com/pod-product-compliance
Lightning Source LLC
Chambersburg PA
CBHW031454160726

47994CB00005B/2023